The Curse of the Cockers

John and Beth Cunningham are in the pub celebrating Hogmanay with their business partner Isobel Kitts and her husband Henry when they hear a new business proposition. The Cunninghams own Three Oaks Kennels, where they breed and train gun dogs, and Angus Todd, John's sergeant in the Falklands, suggests they join him in running a commercial shoot. Needing time to mull over this option, the Cunninghams return home early. But their plans for a peaceful evening are shattered when a late-night telephone call informs them that Isobel and Henry have been involved in a fatal accident.

Beth rushes to the scene and is relieved to find that her friends are unharmed. A fellow reveller, however, now lies dead, the victim of a hit-and-run driver. The killer was driving a Land-Rover, but further clues are scarce. Could the terrified cocker spaniel found abandoned at the roadside be a possible lead? Until somebody turns up to claim him, the Cunninghams agree to look after the dog at their kennels.

Despite the news of a particularly gruesome murder in the area, the hit-and-run is not something Angus Todd will ever forget. For traces of blood have been found on his Land-Rover's bumper . . . Todd protests his innocence and, in desperation, asks John Cunningham to help him clear his name. But what starts as a favour for a friend develops into a hunt for a double killer, when a vital clue is discovered linking the two deaths. Cunningham follows the trail . . . straight into a nightmarish encounter with a ruthless psychopath.

THE CURSE OF
THE COCKERS

GERALD HAMMOND

St. Martin's Press
New York

Library of Congress Cataloging-in-Publication Data

Hammond, Gerald, 1926–
    The curse of the cockers / Gerald Hammond.
       p.   cm.
    ISBN 0-312-10446-4
    1. Cunningham, John (Fictitious character)—Fiction.
2. Dog breeders—Scotland—Highlands—Fiction.
3. Murder—Scotland—Highlands—Fiction. 4. Highlands
(Scotland)—Fiction. I. Title.
PR6058.A55456C87   1994
823'.914—dc20   93-40477
                                        CIP

First published in Great Britain by Macmillan London Limited.

First U.S. Edition: March 1994
10 9 8 7 6 5 4 3 2 1

ONE

I raised my glass. 'Another ghastly year,' I said, 'drags to its dreary close.'

Beth, my wife, looked at me anxiously. 'That isn't really what you think, is it?' she asked.

Isobel, my other partner, looked at me reprovingly through her spectacles and snorted. 'He always says that. It doesn't mean anything.' Isobel knew me long before Beth came on the scene.

'It's only a saying,' I added quickly. Sometimes Beth takes me too seriously. 'All in all, it's been a damn good year. I'm sorry to see it go.'

That was true. A breeding and training kennels for working spaniels can be a reasonable money-spinner or an easy way to get rid of superfluous cash, depending on management, reputation, and a fair degree of luck. After several sluggish years, during which the books had balanced as precariously as the scales of justice, the luck had turned. A succession of wins at field trials, some of them merited and some not, had brought us the reputation; and we had made some good guesses in deciding the ever vexed question of which puppies to keep for competition and breeding, which to dispose of as pups, and which to train on for sale as trained or half-trained dogs. As a result, our pups now commanded good prices; but there was more profit in bringing on our trained dogs, now very much in demand, and in training for the clients who were beginning to beat a path to our door.

We were happy, but busy. The arrival of a baby boy

could have passed almost unnoticed among so much fecundity – even by Beth, who had been found teaching a group of novices the elements of retrieving on the lawn when young Sam was less than seventy hours old; but in fact his birth had set the seal on my contentment. Life, which I had thought to be over when a serious illness brought a premature end to my army career, looked good again.

'I should think you would be,' Henry said severely. Henry Kitts is Isobel's husband. Although not formally a member of the partnership he had put up Isobel's share of the capital and is a staunch source of aid and good advice. If Isobel is a mother figure in the business, Henry, who is older than Isobel and, although usually as fit as the proverbial flea, looks older still, could be its grandfather.

He leaned back and looked around the bar of the local inn. 'Not very busy, considering the occasion,' he said.

The occasion was Hogmanay, New Year's Eve in Scotland. Even as recently as my boyhood, Christmas was hardly noticed in Scotland; and, when commercial pressure finally forced recognition of it, the Scots were in no hurry to give up their more traditional celebration. Thus the festive season tends to revive just when the stomach and the purse are looking for the end of it.

The long bar, which rambled through the old building, was far from empty but was doing little more than normal business. The local constable had wandered through earlier in the evening, not looking at anybody in particular but in uniform and carrying one of the new electronic breathalysers, and those who had been drawn from a distance by the inn's excellent cuisine and ambience had taken the hint. The serious drinking was confined to those who, like ourselves, lived within walking distance.

'I wonder what the new year will bring,' Beth said quietly.

'More of the same,' I said. 'That's all I ask for.'

'No ambition,' Isobel said. 'That's your trouble. A young man should be looking for new worlds to conquer.'

6

She is always trying to spur me into activity. Beth was ready to protest, I could tell. One of her self-imposed duties is to protect me from any stress which she feels might set my recovery back. I tend to ignore them both when it suits me and go my own way.

Instead, Beth looked past my shoulder. 'Angus Todd's heading towards us,' she said. 'Shall I make faces at him until he goes away?'

I knew what she meant. I liked Angus, but there was no denying that he had a quick temper and, when annoyed, a rough edge to his tongue. He had been my sergeant during the Falklands conflict and now seemed to vacillate between a degree of residual respect and taking a perverse pleasure in slanging off his ex-officer. When it comes to repartee I can give as good as I get, so Angus and I had, on occasions, descended to slanging matches but without any real animosity behind them. After leaving the Army, he had worked as a gamekeeper but was now a game farmer in a small way, breeding a few thousand pheasants a year plus duck and some red-legged partridges. He also acted as a wildfowling guide in winter months.

'It wouldn't work,' I said. 'Angus rather fancies you. He'd think you were giving him a come-on.'

Beth looked surprised and abashed. She is that great rarity, a woman who is usually unaware of being fancied and is quite shocked when forced to notice it.

'Maybe he wants to buy a pup,' Isobel said.

'Very unlikely,' said Henry. 'He already has a golden retriever, with a cocker to do the hunting.'

Angus arrived at our table, very spruce in a stiff-looking new tweed suit. He had brought the army habit of smartness and attention to equipment with him into civilian life, whereas I had opted for comfortable shabbiness. His tubby five-foot-six seemed to tower over us. He was quite sober but seemed to be in his more genial mood. 'What are you drinking?' he asked.

He had a modest half-pint in his hand, but a round of

drinks would have set him back more than a hard-earned fiver. 'We're all right for the moment,' I said, 'but don't ever stop asking us.'

He grinned, but I sensed that he was relieved. I suspected that money was tight. 'Join you for a minute?'

I stretched and pulled a chair from another table and he sat down. 'Yon daft kennel-maid of yours said you were here,' he said. 'She thought you'd be back any minute.'

'Wishful thinking,' said Henry.

'So I jaloused. I was to meet somebody here so I came on down. You're sure you'll none of you have a drink?'

'Quite sure,' Isobel said. I saw Beth's eyebrows going up. It was unlike Angus to be quite so forthcoming or Isobel to be so restrained.

He hummed to himself for a minute and took a sip from his glass. 'It must be a problem to you,' he said at last, 'all those dogs to train and only a wee bit land of your own.'

'Most of the farmers are helpful,' I pointed out.

'Oh aye. But that's ninety-nine per cent rabbit and pigeon. You're training for field trials.'

'If the dogs are steady to rabbits and soft-mouthed with pigeon, they can cope with anything,' Isobel said. 'We do a lot of beating and picking-up.' She spoke hesitantly. There was much in what Angus was saying.

'You can't pick-up outside the season,' Angus said. 'What you need is ready access to land with game birds on it, year in and year out.' He leaned forward and looked at each of our faces in turn. 'There's a very good shoot on the market, not so far from here, at a bargain rental.'

'You're thinking of forming a syndicate?' Beth asked.

He shook his head forcefully. 'There's room for another commercial estate around here. It'd make sense for me to run it. I could supply the birds and do the keepering, and if visitors want more shooting than the ground can stand I could take them after the geese. Would you be interested?'

8

I was about to say not but Isobel spoke first. 'Where exactly would we come in?' she asked him.

'I could no more do the whole thing by myself than fly in the air,' Angus said frankly. He leaned forward, his round face with its fringe of beard taut with eagerness. 'To begin wi', there's the money. The first year's lease would need to be paid soon and I'd have to live until the end of October and feed my birds. Well, my bank manager's daft, but he's not that daft. Then, I'm not great on the managing side – advertising and bookings and accounts and VAT and the likes of that.' (Isobel was nodding. We share the administration but she is the management expert.) 'The visitors would need to be met and taken to their hotel and entertained to dinner.' (Henry began to look interested. Although not officially a member of the firm, I could tell that he was seeing himself in that function.) 'On shoot days, I could look after the beating line if there was somebody to place the guns and do the picking-up.' He looked at me. 'And there's the vermin. That comes just when I'd be busiest with the rearing. If you were visiting the ground regularly to train your springers, you could keep an eye open for foxes and magpies and the like, maybe visit a few snares and feed a call-bird in a Larsen trap.' He looked around our faces again. 'What do you say?'

'Where is this shoot?' I asked him.

Angus shook his head and the visible part of his face took on a stubborn look that I remembered well.

'We're not going to rush in and gazump you,' Isobel said. 'We'd need you as much as you'd need us.'

'Maybe. But things can be let slip. I'd want to know first if you're interested. If you are, I'll tell you soon enough. If not, you've no need to know.'

I opened my mouth to give him his answer, but again Isobel spoke first. 'This is too sudden,' she said. 'We'll need time to think it over.'

'Aye, you will that. But don't take long. The deal needs to be firmed up soon.' He pulled a sheet of paper from an inner pocket. 'I've put down a few figures. I'll leave them with you. We'll be in touch.'

He got to his feet and headed for the bar.

'Well, I don't know,' I said.

'A new world to conquer,' Isobel said. 'We'll have a look at the figures.'

'We've already bitten off as much as we can chew.'

'It needn't involve us in much that we don't do already,' she retorted. 'It could turn a useful profit on its own. And there's no doubt about it, access to ground that's hopping with game birds would give us a flying start when the season opens.'

'My round, I think,' Henry said. 'Same again?'

'We should be going,' Beth said quickly.

'So should we,' said Henry. 'But we've no intention of doing so. The night is young and so are you.'

'We're not as young as we were,' I said. 'And Daffy will want to get down here for a drink with Rex before closing time.'

Daffy – given name Daffodil but always known as Daffy because the contraction was so very suitable – was our new kennelmaid. Beth had originally come to us in that position and had continued to do all the work, and more, after our marriage. But with the approach and arrival of Sam it had been obvious that help would be required and Daffy's had been the only reply to our advertisement. To her other duties had been added occasional baby-sitting. Rex, Daffy's totally unsuitable boyfriend, was propping up the bar and glaring at us. He had a studded leather jacket, a Mohican haircut, and a luminous green stripe in what was left of his hair, but was otherwise unremarkable.

'I doubt if Daffy and Rex would give a damn whether the bar was open or not,' Isobel said. She and Henry were sociable boozers when the mood took them. 'Their only common interest is in fornication.'

'She's very good with the dogs,' Beth said. 'And with Sam. We'd better go.'

'We'll phone you after midnight,' Isobel promised.

We exchanged premature good wishes for the New Year with such familiar faces as we passed on the way to the door and rooted among the coats for my sheepskin coat and Beth's quilted waterproof.

The night welcomed us coldly. An early fall of snow had thawed before Christmas, to the regret of the nostalgic few. There was a stiff breeze and the temperature was hovering around freezing-point. A few degrees colder and the drier air would have had less power to sap away the body's warmth. We walked briskly. When the lights of the village fell behind us, a glimmer from half a mile ahead drew us home.

Home was and is Three Oaks Kennels, a converted farmhouse in about five acres of land, set back from the first bend in the road. The comfort of the house was calling, but duty had the louder voice. We turned away and made a tour by torchlight of the neat groups of kennels and runs. The locks were secure and a variety of snores and dream-noises assured us that all was in order. Several of the younger dogs awoke and stood up against the wire for a quick exchange of greetings or reassurance.

In the hall, we were met by warmth and the familiar atmosphere of the old house. And by Daffodil.

Daffy was definitely an oddball. *Au fond* she was a nice-looking girl although she had a jaw which was firm to the point of being called, on anybody less pretty, obstinate. She came from a good home in Dundee but had walked out after a dispute with her mother over the unsuitable Rex. Her father, a well-heeled businessman whom I knew slightly, was secretly continuing her generous allowance, so that Daffy was not too concerned about the scale of her wages. All that she wanted was a respectable job – this was a condition set by her father on her allowance – and bed and board within reach of Rex. We converted our one uncommitted outbuilding into a bedroom for her and Beth made it clear that while Daffy might be within reach of Rex this particular bed was not.

11

The appointment had turned out surprisingly well. Daffy was a hard worker, loved dogs, and had fallen hard for Sam. Those characteristics, plus a willingness to do the sometimes unpleasant tasks of the kennelmaid for a minute salary, more than made up for a certain eccentricity of style. She was wearing brightly patterned tights and knee-length cycling shorts under a very short skirt. What if anything she was wearing above was concealed beneath a jacket of very hairy synthetic fur. Her fair hair had, as usual, a stripe to match that of Rex. Either they were in telepathic communication or they arranged by telephone to co-ordinate the day's colour scheme. Her lips and eyelids were a similar green.

Sam, Daffy reported, had been fed and changed and was sound asleep. And she would see us in the morning. She bade us a happy New Year – when it came – and was out of the house while her last words were hanging in the air. We heard her pattering down the drive. I knew that she really would be at work in the morning. Daffy, for all her faults, never missed out on the job for lack of sleep or excess of sex, alcohol, or whatever else she might indulge in.

We shed our coats and I followed Beth into the large, bright kitchen. She put the kettle on. 'What did you think Daffy looked like?' she asked.

I gave it a little thought and surprised myself by saying, 'I thought she looked rather good. She shocks the locals out of their wits, but if she went on television like that she'd stand out as a beauty.'

'The locals are used to her by now. It's not fair,' Beth said cheerfully. 'If I tarted myself up like that I'd look like somebody's nightmare.'

'You might not,' I said. 'You could try it and see. You look young enough to get away with it.' Beth was a good ten years older than Daffy but could have passed for her niece.

'Would you like that?'

'No, I don't think I would.'

12

Beth looked at me appraisingly. I thought that she was weighing my answer, but she said, 'You're tired.'

'Not really,' I said, and then spoiled it by yawning.

'Oh yes you are. Go on up to bed and I'll bring us up a hot drink.' Although I was recovering from the parasite that had finished my army career I was still not back to full strength and Beth was often more aware of it than I was.

'We'll just see the New Year in.'

'We'll see it in in bed,' she said firmly. 'Take the phone up with you. If we put the lights out, nobody'll bother us.'

I liked the idea. At midnight on Hogmanay the visiting begins, the first foot over the threshold bringing good luck and receiving suitable hospitality in return. The previous year, we had been rash enough to be caught at home by neighbours and the party had gone on until dawn; but when the house seems dark and silent it is assumed that you are already out doing the rounds – 'first-footing'. I unplugged the phone in the sitting room, carried it upstairs, and plugged it in in the bedroom.

Sam was in his cot, surrounded by all the paraphernalia of babyhood. At four months, he had lost the individuality of the newborn and looked to be just another chubby baby, but he was ours. He was deeply asleep. We had been lucky; after the first few weeks he had turned into a mighty sleeper.

Beth brought up a tray. In addition to the hot drinks were a plate of shortbread and two decorous glasses – a small sherry for herself and a larger, but watered, whisky.

We curled up sleepily together, enjoying a more or less platonic cuddle while listening to the radio playing very softly, and at midnight we sat up, ate the shortbread, and toasted each other solemnly.

The bell was switched off for Sam's sake, but we heard the ringing from the phone in the kitchen and took the extension under the bedclothes with us. My brother in Dunoon wished us a happy New Year. We came up for a few breaths of air and then Beth phoned her mother in Aberfeldy.

'One more,' Beth said softly. 'Henry and Isobel. Then we can go to sleep.' Before we could begin to make the call, we heard the phone ringing downstairs and submerged again. It was my turn to take the phone. 'Happy New Year,' I said.

'The same to you,' said a voice which I couldn't place, a man's. 'Is that Mr Cunningham?'

'Yes.'

'Mrs Kitts asked me to phone you. There's been an accident. Would one of you go down, please? It's just the far side of the village from you.'

Beth had her ear close to mine. She grabbed the phone from me. 'It isn't Henry, is it?'

'I'm afraid I don't know any more than that,' said the voice. The connection was broken.

I flipped back the bedclothes but Beth was out before me. 'Oh no you don't,' she said. 'I'll go. I'm not having you wandering about in the cold and dark.'

'I could take the car.'

'You're over the breathalyser limit by now. And if you go on foot you'll probably get drawn into a ceilidh in somebody's house and end up catching your death. I'll take the car and go and see what's happened.'

'We'll both go.'

'You're staying where you are.'

There is no arguing with Beth when she uses that tone of voice. I relaxed against the pillows. I must have been very tired because, despite my anxiety, I remember nothing between hearing her drive off and feeling a cold body snuggle up against me for warmth.

I managed a small interrogatory grunt.

'They're both all right,' she said. 'I'll tell you in the morning. Nothing for us to worry about.'

Small sounds woke me. The cheerful singing and a crunch of footsteps below the window came from Daffy, already

14

busy with the endless tasks of feeding and cleaning. I opened my eyes. The slurping sound was Sam, sucking greedily at his breakfast bottle. Beth, in her pink dressing-gown, could have been a teenager tending her baby brother.

'Was I dreaming last night?' I asked her.

'No. There really was an accident. But Henry and Isobel weren't involved, except as witnesses.' There was no hint of reproach for my callous sleeping. Beth knows and approves of nature's way of protecting me from any stress that might set back my recovery. 'A man was knocked down in the road, the other side of the village. It was a hit-and-run. They saw it happen. And we have a visitor.'

I was becoming aware of another sound, a shrill yipping from somewhere downstairs. 'What on earth's that noise?' I asked.

'That's the visitor.' Sam had lost interest in his bottle. Beth turned him round to her shoulder and began patting his back. 'A cocker spaniel pup. He came out of the hedge near the accident. Presumably he belonged to the dead man. Isobel didn't trust the police to look after him properly. That's why she phoned. And I think the police were glad to be able to dump him on us for now. I've given him a basket in the surgery for the moment. We don't know what shots he has or hasn't had. He certainly isn't old enough to have had all of them.'

'The accident was fatal, was it? You said "dead". We'll have to contact the relatives and find out what they want done with him.' I rolled over and sat up. 'Time I was moving.'

'You'll find everything for your breakfast beside the stove.'

I got out of bed and wished Sam a happy New Year. My clothes had been warming on the radiator. As I dressed, we could hear Daffy returning. She was singing to the tune of 'Just My Bill', always a sign that she had enjoyed herself the previous night. We could not make

15

out the words, which may have been just as well. Daffy was in the habit of relieving the boredom and at the same time signifying her rebellion against all symbols of her previous existence by putting new and sometimes ribald words to the songs that she associated with home life.

Beth and I often pick up each other's thoughts. 'Rex is never known as Bill, is he?' she asked suddenly.

'It's what the builder said to me when he brought his account,' I said. ' "Just my bill." '

Beth shook with half-suppressed laughter and as I left the room I heard Sam give vent to an enormous burp. 'Good boy,' said Beth. I thought that it would be only a few years before we were trying to teach him not to make that sort of noise.

On my way to the kitchen I detoured to the surgery. This was no more than a small room which had been tiled and equipped so that Isobel, who had begun her working life as a vet, could deal with accidents or infection among our stock.

The yipping stopped as I opened the door. An all-black cocker puppy of about eight weeks was sitting in too large a basket in the corner. He lowered his head and looked at me anxiously. There were a puddle and several messes on the tiled floor. I picked him up. No collar or other identification and no signs of serious injury although two neat stitches had been put in a small cut between his toes. He was a good weight, considering the smallness of the breed, although his stomach felt empty.

Nobody would have given Daffy any orders about him yet. To the tune of renewed yelping, I went to the kitchen and mixed some puppy meal with warm milk. The noise cut off as I re-entered the surgery and when I put the bowl down he dived headfirst into the food.

I was finishing breakfast when Daffy came into the kitchen for more puppy meal. She seemed to have switched allegiance and was now singing 'Come into the garden, Claud'. She still had the coloured stripe in her hair but otherwise, in Wellingtons and dungarees and

16

without the surrealist makeup, she could have passed for a comparatively normal girl. We exchanged New Year greetings and I gave her the traditional dram of whisky. She shot it down her throat with an ease which no young girl should have acquired at her age.

When I mentioned the newcomer, she nodded. 'I was going to ask you about him.'

'I've just fed him. I don't suppose he'll be here for long. For the moment, try him on about two-thirds of the diet we give a weaning springer. He can live in the surgery for now. We're a bit short of isolation kennels.'

She cocked her head and listened to the cries of loneliness and despair from the surgery. 'The noise will drive you mad,' she said. 'But it's no skin off my nose. I can't hear him from my room.'

If she had been in her room, I thought, it could only have been to change her clothes. She had the bruised but complacent look of a woman who has not spent the night in innocent slumber. 'Then he'll have to get used to the great outdoors,' I said. 'He won't take kindly to that. He can't have been away from his dam for more than a few days at the most. But that's his problem. If he wakes Sam in the night, we'll none of us get any sleep.'

Daffy paused at the door, with her pan of steaming meal resting on her hip. 'It would take the hound of the Baskervilles to waken Sam, once he's got off,' she said. 'You heard about the accident last night?'

'That's where the pup came from,' I told her. 'He seems to have been with the man who was knocked down. Mrs Kitts was on the scene. She was roped in as a witness. She got somebody to phone us and Beth went to collect the pup.'

'I think we'd just passed him in the road before it happened,' Daffy said. 'We hoofed out to first-foot Rex's gran and on the way back we passed a man. It was dark, but from the sound of his footsteps he was good and pissed.

'Then, just as we reached the lights of the village, we

17

crossed with Mr and Mrs Kitts on their way home. We heard some noises a minute or two later but we just thought it was somebody buggering about. We heard about the accident later, from Rex's dad. I suppose he staggered out in front of a car. I'd better go, or this meal will be cold.'

As she lugged her burden out, I was treated to the rest of her invitation to the mythical Claud. If Daffy was still with us when Sam reached the age of imitation, she would have to be taught to whistle.

Like most other Scots, we had given ourselves and the dogs a bit of a rest between Christmas and the New Year, but it was time to settle to work before Daffy decided that if she was doing the lion's share of the work she deserved the lion's share of the money. I wrapped up warmly against the day and went outside.

Three owners had left young dogs with us for training and I gave each of those an individual workout with the whistle and a dummy launcher in an adjoining field before turning my attention to our own stock.

The Spaniel Championships were imminent and we were running two dogs. Lob (short for Lobelia) had qualified to run and, with one success already to her name, we hoped for another, to bring her to Field Trial Champion status. Rowan, bought in as a pup from a good strain to introduce new blood, had already gained that distinction through his wins in open trials, but a good result at the championships would enhance his demand and fees at stud. I fetched a gun, some blanks, and some live cartridges and took them in turn to the Moss.

Sam, well tucked into blankets, was in his pram in the garden by the time that that exercise was finished and Beth, one eye on the pram, was busy with another of her self-imposed duties, tidying the garden. Daffy had finished the first round of chores and, for the brief interval before the younger pups had to be fed again, she joined me in exercising and giving elementary training to the younger stock.

18

When we broke for lunch, there was still no sign of Isobel. This was unusual but not unexpected. As the senior partner – in years at least – she allowed herself occasional latitude; and she and Henry, both bibulous by nature, were inclined to look on Hogmanay through the bottom of a glass.

Daffy had caught Beth's habit of treating me as a delicate invalid. They ganged up on me and made me nurse Sam in one of the basket chairs in the kitchen while Beth prepared his feed and Daffy made a quick meal. I sometimes found this excess of matriachy galling but I refused to feel smothered by it. On the many occasions when I was below par, it was a relief to know that I could rest and recuperate without being made to feel I was shirking. Sam was his usual sunny self but determined to get a good grip on my nose. It was not what I had envisaged as a father and son relationship, but it would do for a start.

Isobel arrived twenty minutes later, looking distinctly frayed, and uttered the customary New Year greeting. We responded with rather more conviction. Daffy, whose manners were better than her style, got up at once. 'Have you had lunch?' she asked.

Isobel kissed all four of us before dropping into the vacated chair. 'Not to notice,' she said. 'In fact, I haven't even had breakfast.'

'You're our First-Foot,' I told her. 'If you don't count Daffy—'

'There's no certainty that she could count as high as one at the moment,' Daffy said.

'—So you'll take a dram?'

Isobel gave a ladylike shudder. 'Perhaps in a year or two . . .'

Beth, who had bolted her own snack in order to take Sam for a feed and change, looked up. 'Oh dear. You didn't drive?' she said.

'I'm not daft,' Isobel said. She and Henry lived a mile or two beyond the village, so she often walked over. 'I'd probably still send the breathalyser off the dial.' There was a pause while she tasted her own mouth and seemed to find it less than satisfactory. 'If Sam's left you any milk to spare,' she told Daffy, 'I might manage cereal and coffee with plenty of sugar.'

Daffy put a bowl, milk, a packet of cornflakes, and the sugar basin in front of her. 'You seemed all right when Rex and I left the hotel,' she said.

Isobel laughed without amusement. 'That was then. We hung on until midnight, when the late licence ran out. We sang "Auld Lang Syne", shook hands with friends and strangers alike, and set off. We'd only walked a minute or two when . . . Did I tell you about the accident?'

'You got somebody to phone us,' Beth said. 'I came down to collect the pup.'

Isobel swallowed a mouthful of sweetened cereal and shuddered again. 'God, I'd forgotten about the pup,' she said. 'Yet my memory's fairly clear at that stage. We'd left the pub and turned for home. There's wasn't much light, the moon was hidden by cloud, but we could hear that somebody was walking ahead of us. We heard a vehicle behind us so we stepped onto the verge and cowered in the hedge while a Land-Rover went by, accelerating hard. We had a glimpse of the man, the other pedestrian, in the headlamps. He showed up clearly, sort of frozen in time. He seemed twisted, as though he was trying to jump out of the way but couldn't make up his mind which way to go, and I saw him give a sort of wave. The Land-Rover jigged both ways as though the man's antics had confused the driver. Then there was a thump and we saw the man turn a complete somersault. The Land-Rover slowed and then went off in a hurry.'

'You didn't recognize it?' I asked.

'No. It was a short-chassis Land-Rover, common as muck around here. I think it was the usual olive green but I couldn't swear to it. By the time the accident happened, it was too far off to read numberplates.' Isobel bolted the rest of her cereal. 'I think I may live now,' she said. 'If you can call it living.'

'We'd just crossed with you,' Daffy said. 'We'd seen in the New Year with Rex's grandmother. We called to you. Do you remember that?'

'Of course I do, I think,' Isobel said indignantly.

'We saw a Land-Rover leave the village,' Daffy said. 'We'd no reason to notice it particularly, except that he seemed to be in a bit of a hurry. If it was the same one, I'd agree with you that it was the usual green.'

'Colours look different under street-lamps,' I pointed out.

'You had a better look at it than we did,' Isobel told Daffy. 'You'd better go and talk to the police.

'Anyway, we hurried to where the man was lying. Henry still had a torch with him although the old fool seems to have lost the good pigskin gloves I gave him for Christmas. I stayed with the man while Henry dashed back to the police station, as near as he can come to dashing these days. Not that there was much I could do for the victim. If he wasn't already dead he was on the way out. I think his neck was broken.'

Isobel tasted her coffee, added more sugar, and drank again.

'You're sure you couldn't manage a hair of the dog?' I asked her.

She shook her head, gently. Isobel has her own regime for the day after. 'I could manage it but I couldn't keep it down. I might accept a shandy in about half an hour's time,' she said.

'But who was it?' Beth asked. 'He was already in the ambulance by the time I got there. Not anybody we knew?'

'I doubt it. I saw him for the first time in the bar that evening. You probably noticed him, too. But that doesn't constitute knowing. He was a jolly-looking man but there was something sly about him. He was quite smart in a new checked tweed sports jacket, but he needed a shave. And he was on the scrounge for free drinks.'

'Around fifty years old?' I asked.

'Forty to fifty.'

'We certainly did notice him,' I said. 'Before you

21

turned up, he attached himself to us for a few minutes and chatted on about nothing at all in an accent that was supposed to be refined but which had definite overtones of either Dundee or Glasgow. He bummed a whisky off me and then moved on before we were ready for another round.'

Isobel nodded, with more confidence. 'I saw him doing the same at several other tables. He was having a high old time without ever putting his hand in his pocket,' she said. 'By the time he left, he could hardly find his own coat. And he was only just outside the door when I heard him cry out. I thought that he'd slipped and fallen, but by then I'd decided that he wasn't the sort of man you rush to help.'

Beth had finished with the now comatose Sam. She put him into his pram. 'But what about the puppy?' she asked.

As if in reply, the pup must have woken. The shrill yipping from the surgery resumed.

'I know that voice,' Isobel said. 'I heard it when Henry went off to fetch help. I'd heard it earlier but my mind was taken up with the accident victim and I'd put it down to a rabbit caught by a stoat or something. But when I realized that the man was past helping I also realized that the noise certainly wasn't coming from a wounded rabbit. Henry had left me the torch and I shone it towards the hedge and there was the little beggar sitting and yipping. It—'

'He,' I said.

'He, then. I wasn't much concerned with gender at the time. He stopped when I picked him up and when Henry came back we put him – the pup,' she explained carefully, 'into his, Henry's, pocket and he, the pup, settled down peacefully. Probably hasn't been away from his dam and siblings for more than a matter of hours and doesn't like being alone. It's a very common reaction.'

'Nobody knew whether the pup belonged to the dead man or not, but Henry's pocket didn't seem to be the best place for him and Henry wasn't keen to have his coat pulled out of shape and his pocket piddled in. It looked as though we'd be kept hanging around for ever. General opinion was that the best place for him until somebody turned up to claim him would be here, so I got the first passer-by to phone you.

'The local bobby checked by radio with Cupar and nobody had reported a puppy lost. He was as considerate as he could reasonably be and we got home by about two, fired with good intentions of going straight to bed. But those idiots, the Caldwells, saw our lights on and decided to come first-footing. Before we could get rid of them, two more couples turned up, bringing bottles and other goodies. The party went on until breakfast time. I'm getting too old for that sort of thing,' Isobel added peevishly.

Nobody dared to comment.

Daffy was mixing another bowl of meal for the young puppies' midday feed. She took a dish through to the surgery and came back. The yipping was cut off. 'That puppy couldn't have belonged to the deady,' she said. 'Drunk or sober, he wouldn't have been jay-walking an expensive pup at midnight on a public road without a collar or lead, not unless he was bloody daft.'

'He could have been carrying him home,' Isobel said. 'Perhaps he'd just bought him.'

'Who from?' said Beth. 'There hasn't been a litter of cockers around here for at least a year, maybe two. It's more likely that he had the pup in the car and decided that he'd go for a walk until he was sober enough to drive.'

'That could have taken long enough,' I said.

'Drunks don't realize that,' said Daffy. 'He decided to walk it off. He took the pup along and was too pissed to think about a lead. Is there still an unclaimed car in the inn's car park?'

'I only saw the boss-man's Shogun when I came by,' Isobel said. 'They don't open the bars on Ne'erday. But

I couldn't see round the back and I had no particular reason to look.'

'Either it was something like that or it's pure coincidence,' I suggested. 'Somebody may have dumped an unwanted Christmas present near where the accident was about to happen. The accident may even have happened because the driver was trying to avoid the pup.'

'It isn't the time of year yet for abandoning,' Daffy said. 'Christmas was only a week ago. The novelty wouldn't have worn off yet. Unless the family was going off for a winter break and had just realized that they were going to have the scutter of kennelling the pup and that kennels are pretty fussy about inoculations. That happens sometimes.' She turned and carried her bowl outside.

'Aren't people horrible?' Beth said indignantly.

I stopped myself from nodding agreement. Not all people are horrible. Quite a lot, but not all. 'I know you believe that God should have stopped at gun dogs,' I said, 'but without people none of the present breeds would have happened at all. Anyway, we never sell pups for pets and I always make it clear that if there's a change of heart – if, for instance, the wife puts her foot down – I'll take the pup back. At a discount, of course.'

'Of course. That's you told,' Isobel said to Beth with mock severity. 'Now before getting down to work for another year, I'll have that shandy and take a look at the visitor.'

I brought the shandy to the surgery. Isobel was holding the now silent puppy. 'About eight weeks,' she said. 'His tail's been docked. His ears aren't long enough to trip him up, so I'd say that he's from working or field trial stock, which is becoming unusual these days – cockers seem to have gone out of fashion except for showing and as pets. Hold the glass for me.' I held the shandy out while she took a swallow. 'Better! I might live now, despite all previous prognoses. You noticed the stitches in his foot?'

'Yes. Broken glass, you think?' Glass is the commonest cause of damage to dogs' feet.

24

'I have my doubts. Hold him for me.'

I put the glass down on Isobel's instrument cabinet and took the puppy. He seemed to take comfort from being handled. He was quite unperturbed, nosing my hand and chewing playfully on my fingers as Isobel deftly snipped and removed the stitches. The cut remained closed. 'No need for those any more,' Isobel said, 'and yet the cut doesn't look as if it's more than a day or two old. And it doesn't seem to have gone through the web. More of a superficial scratch, in my book. Why would anybody suture a scratch?'

'To satisfy an over-anxious owner?' I suggested.

'I suppose it's possible,' Isobel said doubtfully.

TWO

The first local newspapers of the new year came out next morning, but reporters and editorial staff alike must have spent the First of January recuperating because the news all dated back to late December. The road fatality was not mentioned; attention was concentrated on a murder which had been discovered close to Dundee on 31st December although it was believed to have been committed on the previous day.

The victim had been identified as Mrs Violet Wentworth and her body had been found at home by her husband. The body was in the bathtub and the lady was said to have drowned. That much was clearly stated. Beyond these facts, it seemed that the police had been more than usually secretive. The reporters had resorted to their customary habit of making bricks without straw.

The victim's age was given as thirty-two. She was, of course, described as a beautiful blonde, although for once, to judge from a photograph apparently enlarged from a snapshot, there seemed to have been some truth in the description. Another photograph showed the house where the alleged murder had occurred to be a new looking bungalow, apparently spacious and probably expensive, in a country setting.

Of the death itself, few details had been given. The police spokesman had not even given a reason why the death was being treated as murder. Unless more information had been leaked or given under embargo, the reporters were probably drawing inferences from what was left unsaid and the expression on the spokesman's face. The word 'sadistic' appeared several times in the text. In desperation to fill the vacuum, parallels were drawn with another unsolved Dundee case now five years old in which a young motorcyclist had been crippled and left to die of exposure. The similarity, if any, seemed remote.

It was an unpleasant note to start the new year and I turned my mind away to other things.

Unlike many of his kind (who seem obliged to address members of the public much as a headmaster would speak to a small boy who was certainly guilty of something even if it had not yet come to light) I had found Constable Peel to be human and friendly without being any the less conscientious. The police in general also tend to suspect a cheerful public. The theory seems to be that anyone happy must have got away with something. Peel, on the other hand, was a cheerful young man, more inclined to take a second look at anyone showing signs of stress.

Beth – and I to a lesser degree – had been able to help him with a case which had resulted in his being covered in glory. We understood that his sergeant's stripes were not far off. I was delighted when he was detached from Cupar to occupy the police house and station in the village. He was a thin man with a faintly Irish accent and a manner which had remained placid even during the arrest of a violent criminal.

He walked up from the village that afternoon, disdaining the use of the Ford Escort supplied by the Constabulary, greeting each of us with a handshake and New Year wishes and asking after my health and the state of the business. These courtesies over, he settled with Beth and myself in the sitting room. I put a match to the fire.

'I can't offer you a drink?' I asked him.

'You carry on.' He looked at his watch. 'I'm on duty for the next half an hour.'

'Before you go, then.' I took a beer and poured a

27

sherry for Beth. 'Just to fill in the time, what can we do for you?'

He produced a notebook and a ballpoint pen. 'It's about the road traffic fatality at Hogmanay. I already have statements from Mrs Kitts and Miss Macrae.' (Miss Macrae, I remembered, was Daffy.) 'We're interviewing everybody who may have seen the dead man in the inn that night.'

I noticed his choice of words. 'You think that it may not have been an accident?' I asked.

'What put that into your mind?'

'You said "fatality", not "accident",' I reminded him.

He nodded, looked at me consideringly for a moment and then decided that we had been helpful in the past and might be so again. 'We just don't know,' he said. 'This is just between ourselves. Mr and Mrs Kitts were adamant that they never saw brake lights come on. Well, brake lights sometimes fail, but there were no skid-marks in the road. The chiefs are of the opinion that the driver may have been looking down, fiddling with his radio or looking for the end of his seat-belt, just before the impact, and then, because he knew that he'd be in dire trouble if his breath was tested, drove on. So us Indians – that's to say myself and a sergeant from Cupar – are left to look into it.'

'We thought that the driver might have been trying to avoid the puppy,' I said.

'That's no more than a possibility.'

'But we didn't see anything,' Beth said. 'By the time I went down there the ambulance was leaving and you had cones all round everything.'

'That's so.' Constable Peel nodded approvingly. 'But we're trying to interview everybody who was in the bar that night. The vehicle may have come from there and we want to find out all we can about the dead man. Mrs Kitts tells us that you had spoken with him. Did he cadge a drink from you?'

I nodded. 'The oldest ploy in the world,' I said, 'and

quite blatant about it. He was carrying an almost empty glass. He chatted us up, spoke of the weather, asked us what we did, and seemed very interested in the dogs. I could hardly not include him in the next round, after which he spotted another couple whose glasses were nearly empty, pretended to see somebody he knew at the other end of the bar, and slipped away.'

'That seems to have been his usual *modus operandi*,' Peel said. 'What time did you leave for home?'

'About a quarter to eleven.'

'Can you tell me who was still in the bar when you left it?'

He had a list compounded from the statements that had already been taken and as we dug into our memories he marked little symbols against the names. 'I'm afraid we're not being much help,' I said at last. 'Apart from Angus Todd, the ones we knew all live within walking distance and not one of them has a Land-Rover.'

'But any one of them may remember somebody else. That puppy now,' Peel said. 'The man was a stranger around here and it hardly seems likely that he'd been travelling with a young and expensive puppy. You've no idea where else it could have come from?'

We exchanged a blank look. 'No idea at all,' I said. 'Of course, although the pup looks pure-bred it's not easy to tell at that age. If it was the result of an accidental mating, it might not be valuable at all. You've still had no reports of a puppy missing?'

'There's been nothing reported in Fife. We're waiting to hear back from Tayside.'

'I just don't understand,' Beth said. 'He was scrounging his drinks and yet he couldn't have been badly off. He was quite smartly dressed.'

Peel looked at his watch. I glanced at mine and saw that the half-hour was up. 'If your shift's over,' I said, 'you could take a drink now.'

'You're very kind. A beer, then.'

I gave him a beer and topped up our glasses. 'Have you identified him yet?' I asked.

29

Peel put away his notebook. Clearly, he was now off duty. 'You'll treat this as confidential?' he asked.

We said that of course we would.

'Considering the time of year, we've got a long way forward. There was no identification on him. As a first routine step, Kirkcaldy checked his fingerprints and then wired them to other forces. It turns out that he had a record a mile long, but nothing very serious. Sneak-thief, shoplifter, and living by his wits generally. There are a thousand like him, though he was better at it than most.

'He belonged in and around Glasgow but he'd pulled a fiddle on some hard men thereabouts and he was moving around the country while he waited for the heat to cool.

'You say, Mrs Cunningham, that he didn't seem short of a pound or two. He had less than a fiver on him. He was well dressed, you say. He had on a new sports jacket. That jacket had the label of a Dundee store, one of the few that doesn't have the new electronic tags. The staff of the store found a similar jacket, but wrinkled and grubby, hanging among the new ones.'

'You mean,' Beth said, 'that he'd tried on the new one in the fitting room and then hung up the old one in its place and walked out?'

'Just that. His boots were the leather safety boots the oil companies hand out and never recover. They look smart enough.' Peel smiled suddenly. 'I could be doing with a pair myself. I have a cousin that works offshore, but both my feet would go into one of his boots. It isn't true what they say about policemen.

'When he died, the man was wearing a good Barbour coat not more than a few months old. Pinched off a coat-rack somewhere, I've no doubt. Appearances are important to the likes of him. Nobody trusts a scruff.'

'I see that,' Beth said, but she was looking puzzled. If anyone ever produces a league table of the most honest people in the world, Beth's name will certainly figure among the top ten, so the concept of somebody who lived entirely by defrauding others was a foreign language to her.

Now that the formal questioning was over, Constable Peel lay back in his chair, ready for a good chat. I accepted this at face value, but I knew that some policemen expect to gather more hard facts and useful suggestions during a cosy gossip over the teacups when guards are down than by any amount of hectoring.

'For an example,' he said, 'he had had a good dinner at the inn. He collected his bill but, before going to the desk and settling it, he moved through into the coffee room and had coffee and collected another bill for that. Guess which bill he paid.'

'The coffee?' Beth said, round-eyed.

'Right.'

The dead man's character as a petty crook seemed irrelevant. 'Did Mrs Kitts tell you about the stitches in the puppy's foot?' I asked.

'She did. That's another thing makes us doubt that the pup was to do with him. He wasn't the sort of man to pay a vet good money for no good reason.'

'I wouldn't be so sure of that,' I said. 'I once knew an old lady who grudged heating her house on her pension. In cold weather, she lived in perpetual danger of hypothermia. Her family were worried about her. Even when they gave her the money, she wouldn't spend it on heat. So they bought her a budgerigar and told her that she mustn't on any account let the budgie get cold or it would die. After that, the house was always warm. People are funny where their pets are concerned.'

'That's true,' said Peel. 'And not only about their pets. I remember putting one young thug away. His only concern was for his cat.'

'Isobel didn't think that the cut was worth stitches,' Beth said.

'So she told us. But how much weight would you put on that?'

'Some,' I said. 'But you can't always tell. A clean cut can heal up very neatly sometimes. You could ask around the vets and find out whether one of them wasn't stuck with a bad debt. Perhaps the man was supposed to pay when he brought the pup back to have the stitches removed.'

'Now, that's a thought,' Peel said. He dug out his book and made a note. 'If you have any more thoughts like that, pass them along. Especially if they're about cocker spaniel puppies.'

'Why especially that?' asked Beth.

Peel hesitated and then shrugged. 'You'll be reading about it in the *Courier* in a day or two anyway. You saw about the woman who was drowned in Dundee?'

'We saw what it said in the *Courier*,' I told him. 'Half a page of guesswork and about two lines of fact.'

'There's a lot they were keeping back. It was a bad business. She was tied up, good and tight, and left in the bath with the plug in place and the cold tap dribbling.'

We fell silent while we digested the news. All murder is evil but there are degrees of evil; and this was repugnant beyond any conceivable norm. No wonder that the reporters had divined enough to categorize it as 'sadistic'.

'There's more,' Peel said. 'A black cocker spaniel puppy was found in the house, kicked or crushed to death. As far as the nearest neighbour knew, it didn't belong to the dead woman. That scrap of news will be released tomorrow, in the hope that somebody's missing a pup or noticed one that vanished. Of course, Tayside Police were on to us in minutes when they heard about another spaniel puppy being found at the scene of a death. But it's hard to see how the two could be connected.' He smiled crookedly. 'A mad spaniel breeder, perhaps, leaving pups at the scenes of his crimes?'

'All spaniel breeders are mad,' I said. 'They have to be, to go in for anything so risky and such hard work. But we're not as mad as that. Another beer?'

'Well . . . I wouldn't say no.'

I opened another can of beer for him and added a log to the fire. 'Was there anything out of the ordinary in his pockets?' I asked.

He made a face. 'That depends on what you consider ordinary. He had much what you'd expect for a man of his trade. Several credit cards, none of them in his own name – which was Dinnet, by the way. Odds and ends. Some pieces of costume jewellery. Quite a few unidentifiable keys. Two lighters and three packs of cigarettes of different brands. A pair of pigskin gloves, property of Mr Henry Kitts.'

'Isobel told us that the man – Dinnet, was it? – seemed to be having trouble finding his own coat,' I said.

'Going through the pockets for what he could find,' Peel said.

'I suppose . . .' Beth began.

'Yes?'

'I suppose he didn't find more than was good for him?'

Peel gave her a nod and a smile. 'We wondered the same thing. And, in fact, there was a mildly compromising letter tucked into the bottom of a pocket. But there were no names and no address, so I can't see anybody being overly worried about it. *Darling, come and see me tonight. The old man will be away.* That sort of thing. Comparatively innocent in this day and age.'

'Certainly nothing to run a man over for,' I said. 'Unless, of course, the late Mr Dinnet happened to know who wrote it and to whom. Backed by a handwriting expert and if one of those keys happened to fit the wrong door, it could add up to valuable evidence in a divorce case.'

'But most people seem not to worry about divorce any more,' Beth said.

'A wealthy husband with a greedy wife might worry himself sick about it,' I pointed out.

Beth gave the matter some thought. 'Oh well,' she said at last, 'you're not rich and I'm not greedy. How do you suppose he got his hands on the Barbour coat?'

Peel looked at her in puzzlement. 'Any way except by legitimate purchase. As I said, he probably lifted it off a coat-rack somewhere.'

'And have you checked to see if there isn't an unclaimed coat still hanging in the bar?'

The Constable sat up suddenly and then slowly relaxed

again. 'No, we haven't. And if he happened to take a fancy to a good coat and walked off with it . . . and the rightful owner didn't make a squawk about it . . . that could open up what they call – what's that expression they use on the telly?'

'A whole new can of worms?' I suggested.

'That's the one.'

'Well, here's another can-opener,' Beth said. She cocked an ear and when I listened I could hear Sam beginning to whimper for his bottle and a frenzied yipping from the surgery. Beth sighed and got out of her chair. 'Two more hungry mouths to feed. Have you checked the handwriting of that letter to see whether it belongs to the murdered woman?'

She hurried out of the room.

Peel stared at me with his mouth open.

When I walked back from the Moss on the following afternoon, the local Ford Escort police car or one very like it was standing by the front door, making my old estate car look very shabby. A figure in police uniform with sergeant's stripes – a burly figure, verging on stout – was leaning over the pram. My approach across grass was silent. He was making chirruping noises.

One of the two dogs at heel made a faint chuffing sound, the faintest vestige of a bark, as if he knew that I was already aware of the man's presence but instinct demanded that he give me a warning anyway. At the sound, the Sergeant straightened up, turned, and glared at me.

'Captain Cunningham?'

'Mr Cunningham,' I said. I see no need for anybody below the rank of general to carry a military rank into civilian life.

'Sergeant Gall.'

'From Cupar?'

'Yes.' He glared at me suspiciously. 'Do I know you?'

'It was a guess,' I said. 'Constable Peel told me that he

34

was working in harness with a sergeant from Cupar.'

'That young man talks too much. I was hoping for a word with yourself and Mrs Cunningham.'

'If the pram's here, Beth won't be far away. Let me kennel this pair and I'll be with you in a minute.'

He nodded graciously.

As I came back from the kennels I met Beth and Daffy who were returning by way of a track which leads into the adjoining farmland. They were accompanied by two brood bitches at heel and what seemed like a myriad of puppies on leads. The puppies were were busily turning their leads into knitting. (A major problem around a big kennels is the difficulty of keeping the area clean. We tried very hard not to allow the pups to have free-running exercise until the lawns were spotless or until they had reached clean grass or stubble in the neighbouring fields. The habit of eating faeces is too easily contracted in puppyhood and almost impossible to eradicate. Quite apart from the danger of picking up parasites, it is not a habit which impresses the new owner.)

Beth handed her share of the leads to Daffy and came with me. 'I've only been away a minute,' she said defensively, 'helping Daffy to bring the pups back from the field. The track's too muddy for the pram. I could hear her cussing the puppies for running round her legs and I could see you in the distance, heading for home. If I could see you, you could see the house.'

'I was paying more attention to the two dogs I had with me,' I said. 'I missed seeing a car arrive. Where was Isobel?'

'She's taken Henry's car and gone for another load of puppy-meal.'

'Not to worry. Sam's been well guarded,' I said as we arrived back at the front door.

I introduced her to Sergeant Gall and we led him indoors, manoeuvring the pram as we went. The Sergeant's manner was still stiff. Evidently I was not easily to be forgiven for catching him crooning over a baby. I led the way into the kitchen. He would find it more difficult to be formal in the large, jolly room with its scrubbed table and basket chairs than in the sitting room.

Beth had her own and better way of making the Sergeant unbend. She left the pram in the hall, set me to warming a bottle which could as easily have stood in its pan of hot water on the table, and dumped Sam on the Sergeant's knee.

'Hold this thing, please, while I fetch the Carricot,' she said. So the Sergeant sat opposite me, in the other basket chair, looking outraged and yet absurdly gratified, while Sam pulled at the buttons on his tunic, until Beth came back and relieved him.

'Now,' Beth said. She checked the temperature of the bottle. Sam latched onto it like a homing missile. 'You wanted to see us about something?'

Even seated at ease in the homely room, the Sergeant had recovered his air dignity. 'Constable Peel showed me your statements – which I've brought for your signature. He also told me of certain suggestions made by yourselves.'

'You needn't try to sound as though they were indecent suggestions,' I said. 'They were well intended.'

The Sergeant ignored my flippancy. 'I would like to know what put them into your heads.'

'Not guilty knowledge, if that's what you're thinking,' I told him. I could see that Beth, like myself, was in a quandary. We had no desire to drop Constable Peel in the mire by revealing all of his disclosures. 'How much of our discussion did he pass on to you?' I asked carefully.

But for his dignity, I think that the Sergeant would have smiled. He knew perfectly well why we were hedging and he sympathized without approving. 'If it's of any help, he was as frank with me as he admits having been with yourselves.'

'Very well,' I said. 'You had a dead pedestrian. Ostensibly an accident, but you had certain doubts, and rightly so from what we've heard. But why would anybody want

36

to run over a relatively harmless sneak-thief? One possible reason occurred to us. If he was in the habit of renewing his clothes by theft, he might have stolen the wrong coat from the inn, a coat with something damning in the pockets.'

'And the handwriting?'

Beth, who had seemed to be wholly intent on Sam, looked up. 'If it was the way John said, it would have to be something awful. I mean, the letter of assignation on its own needn't have meant much, with no names and so on. Of course, it could have been something else, like a latchkey to a . . . a love-nest. But again, that might have been awkward but not as bad as all that. I mean, let's suppose for a moment that John had a . . . a bit on the side.' Beth turned pink and looked down at Sam. 'I'm sure he hasn't, but if he had; John, would you kill somebody to prevent me finding out?'

That seemed to me the kind of question to which every answer is wrong. 'You can't expect me to tell you in front of the Sergeant,' I said. 'Anyway, I'm not the sort of person who could kill lightly.'

'You must have killed, when you were in the Army,' she said.

'In the line of duty. And even then, not lightly.'

Beth seemed satisfied with my answer. 'There are you. Then I remembered the murder in Dundee. If the letter was in the dead woman's writing, then that might make all the difference. He wouldn't be protecting the secret of his affair, he'd be avoiding a charge of murder. That made a lot more sense. What you've done once comes more easily next time. Were our guesses good?'

'Of course they were,' I said. 'Otherwise, the Sergeant wouldn't be so concerned about how we had so much guilty knowledge.'

'Apparently guilty.' Sergeant Gall made a huffing sound which might have been a sigh. 'As simple as that!' he said. 'Look at it that way round and it's obvious. And yet we'd missed it.'

'You'd have thought of it soon enough,' Beth said.

The Sergeant accepted the comfort reluctantly. 'I don't know that we would. Of course, we're not detectives, just beat coppers investigating a traffic accident. All the same . . .

'There was an unclaimed macintosh with a Glasgow label hanging in the inn, the pockets absolutely empty. The handwriting on the note matches the dead woman's and one of her woman friends claims to recognize one of the pieces of junk jewellery, although she admits that the brooch is hardly unique. A key in the dead man's pocket fitted her front door. Tayside Police are getting excited and my bosses are agitating for a report. One of them will be taking over.' He paused for several long seconds before deciding to abandon his dignity altogether. 'It would look better if we had a tidy theory to present him with. How do you see it?'

I countered his question with one of my own. 'Where would he have been heading for? He'd have needed a bed for the night.'

He hesitated and then made a gesture that might have been a shrug. 'From what Strathclyde sent us, Dinnet never had a permanent abode. He didn't mind sleeping rough but he rarely had to. Sometimes he took a room at a hotel and slipped away without paying the bill – but the man wouldn't have hung around the inn after skipping out on his dinner bill. He's been known to wander into a hotel, find an empty room, slip the lock, and kip down for the night. Other times, when he's been travelling, he's sometimes knocked on a door in some lonely place and passed himself off as a motorist who's broken down a mile or two off. Or he might just sleep in a barn. Sometimes he'd hitch a lift through the night and sleep in the passenger seat of the vehicle.'

'No particular destination, then,' I said. 'He'd treated himself to a good dinner and a lot of drink, all without paying for more than a coffee. Now he was going to move on. He was heading south, away from Dundee and in the general direction of Glasgow.'

'Going home, maybe,' said the Sergeant. 'The men who chased him out of Glasgow have other worries at the moment.'

My vague ideas had firmed up. 'Isobel – Mrs Kitts – told us that she saw him give a sort of wave. Perhaps he was trying to thumb a lift.

'Before leaving the inn, while pretending to look for his own coat, he went through the pockets of the coats hanging there. If he was lucky, he recovered the cost of his coffee – men often carry coins in a coat pocket for car parks and bridge tolls. He pinched Henry's gloves. Then he took the best coat of about his own size and slipped away.

'Minutes later, the owner of the coat prepared to leave. He found that his coat had vanished and he remembered that in its pocket was the letter from the murdered woman and her door key.'

'A careless murderer, to be carrying the letter with him,' the Sergeant commented.

Beth, who had been listening in silence, looked up suddenly and shook her head. 'I think a man who'd only cheated on his wife would have got rid of the note without fail. But if he'd killed his ladyfriend he would have other things on his mind. Guilt, regret, fear. He might be too shaken up to remember to empty his pockets, until his coat went missing.'

'That could be right,' I said. 'The coat's owner may have seen Dinnet fumbling through the coats, so he could guess who he was looking for. He probably only intended to demand his property back, When he saw that Henry and Isobel were following Dinnet and not far behind, he only had a second or two to make up his mind. He made the wrong decision. The sensible thing to have done would have been to drive on and wait for him at the roadside further on. But, in the panic of the moment, he made a mistake.'

The Sergeant was nodding but Beth was shaking her head again. I raised my eyebrows at her.

'If Dinnet had been trying to thumb a lift,' she said, 'that would have made it easy for the other person. He'd only have had to pick him up, drive a bit, and then stop and threaten him until he got his coat back. Dinnet didn't look like a hard man to me and he wouldn't have had time to look at the letter.

'Also, Isobel said that they stepped aside into the hedge when they heard the Land-Rover coming. The driver may not have seen them until he caught sight of them in his mirror against the lights of the village. Until then, he'd expected to be able to stop and recover his things. And you haven't explained the puppy.'

I just looked at her. Sometimes I find myself unsure whether Beth is being dim or brilliant.

'You can explain the puppy?' asked the Sergeant.

'I think so,' she said. 'Listen.' But she fell silent.

We listened. 'I don't hear anything,' Sergeant Gall said.

'Exactly.' Beth still had Sam on her knees and she spoke almost absently while attending to his hygiene. 'Remember the Sherlock Holmes story? The dog that didn't bark? The pup's stopped that yipping now. He's accepted that the surgery is his home and that he'll be fed and visited and looked after. Which goes to confirm that he had only just been separated from his dam and his litter-mates. Yet he settled down quietly in Henry's pocket. That's normal behaviour,' she explained to the Sergeant. 'Dogs are pack animals. Puppies often find aloneness a terrifying experience until they get used to it. They're quite sure that they're being abandoned and left to starve. A pocket probably reminds them of the womb.'

'I understand.'

'When Dinnet left the inn, Isobel thought that she heard him cry out, just after he'd got outside.'

'She thought that he might have slipped,' I said.

'There wasn't any ice. But wouldn't you make a loud exclamation if you put your hand in a pocket and felt something warm, furry, and moving?'

'Wow!' I said. When I thought about it, I found that

I was beginning to catch up with her reasoning. 'By your theory, then, the other man had the puppy with him in the Land-Rover. He was visiting the inn and he didn't want to leave the pup in the car, either because it would chew things or make messes or because its yelping would attract attention that he didn't want. So he took it in his pocket. Barbours have large pockets for carrying shot game and cocker spaniel puppies are comparatively small. The pup fell comfortably asleep and stayed that way. It was warm in the bar and he felt that it was safe to take his coat off and hang it on one of the hooks. But Dinnet helped himself to it, not wasting time on a search but hoping that the weight in the pocket would turn out to be something valuable. Is that it?'

'Just about,' Beth said. She put the sleepy Sam down in his Carricot and faced us again. 'When Dinnet found that he had somebody else's puppy, he could have put the pup down and walked off. But he didn't. He'd drink taken and it was Hogmanay and he was probably glad of some company. Pups aren't the only creatures to feel loneliness. Dinnet walked on, possibly nursing the pup in his hands. I think that, underneath it all, Mr Dinnet may have been a good sort of man.'

'Why on earth would you think that?' I asked her.

'When Isobel saw him make a gesture that was like a wave, he had already seen that the Land-Rover was coming at him. In an emergency like that, people react in funny ways. Instead of trying to save himself, I think he was tossing the puppy into the hedge, out of harm's way. Not everybody would do that.'

'Your instinct would be to do exactly that,' I said.

'And yours.'

'Really? Me, I'd have dived headfirst into the hedge,' said the Sergeant, 'and remembered the puppy afterwards.'

'But you're not a sneak-thief with a low self-esteem,' Beth said. 'Perhaps he had a momentary revelation and realized that he valued himself lower than the pup.'

41

THREE

Another and brighter day, but colder. In the afternoon, frost still sparkled on the leaves of the evergreens and our breaths steamed in the low sun.

'. . . little or no reasoning power,' I said. 'A dog's form of knowledge is: "This is what we always do." Change "always" to "sometimes" and he'll try to think for himself and you may not like what he thinks.

'Now,' I said sternly. 'Before you go, give me some feedback. What are the high spots of what I've been telling you?'

Allan Forsyth looked up from fussing with his spaniel and regarded me timidly. Months before, he had bought a pup from us and had made a mess of the training. So he had brought the young dog back to me and it had taken me two more months to eradicate the bad habits engendered by an indulgent and impatient owner. I was not angry with him. In such cases I overcharge disgracefully, so that sloppy owners are bread and butter to the firm. But because I liked him I was speaking to him severely for his own good.

'Every walk is a training walk,' he said obediently.

We had to move to let a large and sleek but muddy Jag slide towards the front door. 'On which . . .?' I persisted.

'Repeat all the basic exercises.'

'Especially?'

'Sit to the stop whistle. Stay. Come. Heel.'

'And when you feed him?'

'Make him sit until he's told to take it.'

42

'That's to remind him who is the pack leader. What else?'

'Don't shoot over him for at least a fortnight, preferably more. Is that really necessary?' Allan asked plaintively. 'The syndicate's last shoot will be over by then, except the keeper's day.'

'So much the better,' I told Alan. 'Go to the shoot by all means, but if you take the dog leave the gun behind. Keep up the basic training all summer. Shoot a few rabbits for him but stop immediately if he shows any sign of running in. He's still impetuous and he's inclined to be headstrong. I warned you about that before you bought him. You've got to keep on top of him.'

'I'll remember,' he said. But as he drove off I could see the dog leaping around inside of the Land-Rover like a demented squirrel and I was sure that both my training and my good advice would soon be forgotten.

The Jag's driver had got out of the car. He was a large man, somewhere in his forties. His face was bland but something in his manner, a hint of latent self-confidence, made me think that he might be one of the senior policemen foretold by Sergeant Gall. On the other hand, his clothes looked too expensive even for a chief superintendent, if the matter merited such seniority.

He was looking with amusement in the direction of Allan Forsyth's departing Land-Rover. 'You're on a loser, trying to educate that young man,' he said. His accent was good, what would have been called BBC before the Beeb decided that regional accents were 'in'. 'The dog knows exactly who's the master, and it isn't the man. What's more, I'll bet that dog's seriously overweight by next season.'

I knew better than to comment on one client to somebody who I hoped would become another, but I admitted to myself that this man was a judge of human and canine behaviour. Allan's springer had been as fat as a pig when brought back for retraining.

'Can I help you?' I asked. 'I'm John Cunningham.'

43

'My name's Morgan. I've been thinking of getting another spaniel pup to train for the gun. You seem to be getting more than your fair share of champions and I was reminded of where you are when I saw your name in the papers this morning. Something about a fatal accident to a jewel thief, wasn't it? You're looking after the dead man's pup?'

The police made a song and dance about the puppy in the hope of bringing out a clue as to where the pup had come from, but I had been annoyed when they released the name of the kennels. We had had trouble in the past over dogs which had come into our keeping through unconventional channels. 'That was a temporary arrangement,' I told him. Which was true as far as it went. 'Are you looking for a dog pup, or a bitch?'

'I've always preferred dogs. And as young as possible. If that cocker pup's looking for a good home . . .'

'It isn't. We've a litter of springers of about the right age, and there's one dog pup not spoken for.'

'Shy or pushy?'

'He was the pushiest of the litter, but that isn't saying much. His dam's one of those anxious to please bitches and his sire's no extrovert. I expect him to turn out well.'

'Let's take a look at him.'

Beth had come to the front door to be sure that I wasn't getting cold, but I was more than warm in my sheepskin coat and I glared at her to tell her so. She grinned at me and vanished.

I gave Mr Morgan the guided tour of the kennels. It always amuses me when I see hard-boiled businessmen go mushy over young pups and although he tried to look calm and dispassionate I could see that Mr Morgan would have liked to go down on his knees and play. But he knew what he was about and I was in no doubt that any pup of his would be well looked after. He made the acquaintance of the uncommitted dog pup and they seemed to strike up an instant rapport, but he asked some penetrating questions about hip scores and hereditary eye defects.

44

'I'll hand you over to Mrs Kitts,' I said. 'That's her department and she makes sure we don't breed in any future problems. She'll tell you about shots and give you the pedigree. He's registered as Poplar but he won't be worried if you call him something else.'

I left Mr Morgan with Isobel, who had been catching up with the accounts indoors. She must have satisfied him, because I met him on the doorstep twenty minutes later, carrying the pup.

'You took him?' I said. 'I hope you'll be happy together. Do you have a basket for him? And puppy-meal?'

'We'll get by.'

'Will he be far away?' I asked. Morgan looked at me quizzically. 'I like to know where my pups are going,' I explained.

'Not far from Invergordon.'

'You've a long run ahead of you then. I'd better not keep you.'

He nodded and got into the Jag, putting the pup into a small travelling basket on the seat beside him. The car rolled away with a gentle purr that made me envious. My old car sounded as though it was carrying a load of empty beer-cans.

I turned towards the front door.

'He was pulling your pisser,' said a voice.

I jumped and turned round. A deep shrubbery runs along the roadside wall and at the nearest corner, separated from the house by thirty yards of lawn, grew an ancient holly still bright with berries. Inside its dark leaves and almost hidden from view, Rex was sitting at ease on a bare limb. He was warmly wrapped in a leather coat that looked as if it might once have belonged to a Panzer Oberléutnant and the stripe in his hair was now scarlet.

'What the hell are you doing in there?' I asked him.

'Waiting for Daffy to come off. That chiel never comes from Invergordon. I seen that car a dozen times in Dundee, and him driving it.'

I could think of several explanations. Mr Morgan might

45

live near Invergordon but visit Dundee regularly on business. All the same . . .

'Did you notice the registration?'

He shook his head impatiently. 'Plates was too muddy. Looked like he done that a-purpose.'

'I don't suppose it matters,' I said.

I found Isobel in the kitchen. She had returned to her accounts. 'Did you get that man's name and address?' I asked her.

'You told me his name, so that's what I wrote in the forms. I thought you'd taken his details.'

'Let's have a look at his cheque.'

'He paid cash.' Isobel handed over a useful small wad of notes. 'You'd better lock it up for the night. He said that he could trust us, he didn't need a receipt. Is something wrong?'

'I shouldn't think so,' I said.

An hour or so later, the promised senior officers arrived. While I got out of my muddy boots and outdoor clothing, washed, and tried to give myself a veneer of presentability, Beth chatted to them about nothing in particular. They probably thought (as I did) that she was afraid to leave them alone in the sitting room in case they pinched one of our very few heirlooms.

They turned out to be two detective chief inspectors with a detective sergeant in tow. The combination seemed unusual – among the police, as in other large organizations, equal rivals at the top of a pyramid are rarely tolerated, a single figurehead being preferred with the ranks proliferating downwards. I let my surprise show and I was told, in tones which suggested that it was none of my damn business and that Joe Public only existed to speak when spoken to, that one DCI and the sergeant were from Kirkcaldy, the seat of our local police headquarters; the other DCI, who explained carefully that he was only present as an observer, had come over from Tayside. So the likelihood of a link with one or both of the Dundee cases was being taken seriously.

46

Detective Chief Inspector Kipple – from Kirkcaldy – did most of the talking. He went over our previous statements, concentrating on who we had seen at Hogmanay, when, where, and doing what. The sergeant took copious notes, interrupting occasionally to check the spelling of names although these had been checked carefully before our previous statements had been signed. We were then invited to retire to the kitchen while Isobel, and Henry who had walked over to escort her home, were questioned and cross-questioned separately. (We learned later that Daffy and Rex had already been intercepted and milked of their stories.)

Before the police contingent departed, the Tayside DCI, McStraun by name, took a close look at the puppy but he said nothing except to ask whether we were willing to keep him safe for a little longer.

I said that we were, but Beth, who has a sharper eye to the financial side, asked politely who we should bill for the puppy's keep. DCI McStraun looked mildly amused and said that that would, no doubt, sort itself out in due course.

They drove away into darkness, no blue lights flashing.

It was time for an end to the working day and, as usual, we settled for a drink in the sitting room, the three partners plus Henry, with Sam snoring gently on Beth's lap.

'That was rather odd,' I remarked after I had handed round the glasses. 'I don't know what they asked you, but they didn't ask us the questions I'd have asked if I'd been investigating.'

'You mean, if you'd been investigating a total mystery,' Isobel said.

'What my better half means,' said Henry, 'is that they were only mildly interested in descriptions of the few strangers in the bar that night. And they weren't much concerned about the truly local people who would have walked in. They were much more interested in who would have come by vehicle, be it Land-Rover or Reliant Robin Turbo.'

47

'So they're looking for witnesses who'd have been in the car park,' Beth said.

'I think . . .' Henry said slowly. He paused and drank from his whisky. 'I think that they know who they're after and they're looking for witnesses to fill in the gaps in the evidence against him.'

Beth gave a little shiver. 'I hope it's nobody we know,' she said.

'That doesn't matter a damn,' Isobel pointed out. 'If somebody is a serial killer, the sooner he gets his head in a sling the better, whether we know him or not.'

'That's true. And yet you can't help wondering who it is,' Beth said.

'I can,' Isobel said. 'Very easily. Knowing never changes anything, except your peace of mind.'

We did not have to wonder for many hours. Shortly after midnight, I crawled slowly out of a deep sleep to realize that the room was still dark but Beth had vanished from the bed. When I shook off the duvet and raised my head from the pillow I could hear her voice from downstairs. The chill of night was through the house. From the silences, I knew that she was on the phone. I must have dozed again because the next thing I knew was that she was in the room with me, the bedside light was on, and she was plugging in the telephone.

'Just in case it rings again,' she said when she saw that I was awake.

'Who was it?'

Out of habit, Beth took a quick look into Sam's cot before shrugging off her quilted dressing-gown and getting into bed. She wrapped her coldness around me, borrowing warmth.

'Nothing for you to worry about,' she said. 'Mrs Todd was on the phone, wanting to know if Angus was here. Then she wanted to know whether he'd been here at all this evening, because he said he was going to come and see us and he hasn't fetched up at home and she was wondering if he hadn't got himself fu' and set off to walk

48

home again. He does that sometimes. I said that, if he'd had too much to drink here, one of us would have driven him home.'

'We wouldn't have given him that much to drink in the first place,' I said.

'No. But I couldn't tell her that. I said that he was probably walking home from somewhere else and he'd turn up soon. Do you think he'll be all right?'

There was no way I could know whether Angus would be all right or not, but the middle of the night was not the best time for debating the question. I said that I was sure that Angus would get home safely. We were soon asleep again but even in my sleep I knew that Beth was restive.

I was up and about next morning at an hour that was, for me, unusually early, while Beth was still dealing with the demands of Sam and Daffy was beginning the chores. Knowing that the Todds were unvarying early risers, I dialled their number while picking my way through a bowl of cereal.

Mrs Todd answered. Yes, Angus had arrived home safely. She evaded my polite questions, thanked me for asking, and hung up on me. It was unlike the normally garrulous lady to be so curt; she was usually a carefully perfect speaker but she had lapsed into the language and accent of her youth. Mrs Todd, I gathered, was very much upset. I supposed that any wife would be upset by a husband who looked on the whisky while it was amber and had to walk home through the night, and I put Angus out of my mind.

Until, that is, he came creaking and jangling up to the door in the late morning, on a lady's bicycle that must have been at least as old as himself. He was unshaved and looking both ten years older and exhausted – as well he might after such a ride. I had been giving several of the younger dogs steadiness training, at first in the rabbit pen and then on the threadbare grass that passes for our lawn. I left Daffy to kennel them and took Angus out of the cold day and into the warm kitchen, where Isobel was finishing the interrupted accounts and Beth was making preparations for our lunch.

Angus almost collapsed into one of the basket chairs and I took the other. 'What brings you here?' I asked. 'Apart from the bicycle. Have you crashed your Land-Rover?'

He shook his head and stayed silent. This was a far cry from the tough extrovert we knew. Beth gave us each a mug of soup and he nodded his thanks.

'I came . . .' he said at last. 'Came . . . I need to know if you're interested in what I said to you at Hogmanay. I'm tidying up the loose ends. I may be . . .' His voice faded again.

Beth stopped and looked into his face. 'Angus, what's happened?'

Angus glanced at her then met my eyes. 'The police kept my Land-Rover,' he said. 'They've charged me with leaving the scene of an accident, but I've no doubt there's more to come. For the moment I'm on bail.'

'And did you?' I asked him.

He still held my eyes. 'There was no accident that I knew of at the time. I didn't even drive the bugger again that night. Not after I reached the pub.'

'Hogmanay, was that?'

'Aye. I was going easy on the drink, knowing I'd a drive and a long night ahead of me. But after I spoke to you I had a single dram with a mate and then met the man that owns the land the shoot's on. He was on low-alcohol lager but he offered me another dram while we talked business. I said that I'd maybe had enough if I was to drive and he said he'd run me home if I was over the limit. So I took it – a large one – and I bought a round while we were still talking. I was getting a lift, you see?' he repeated anxiously.

'I understand,' I said. 'What went wrong?'

'When we'd tied up some details, I went to the shunkie.

50

I was maybe a bittie longer than I might've been, because Harvey Welcome came in and he was in an awful state for going home, his shirt hanging out and he'd been sick down his front. I couldn't let his wife see him that way so I cleaned him up as best I could and tidied him. When I got back to the bar, the man had given me up and gone. So I had one for the road and set off and walked home.'

'Eight miles?' I said.

'It's not quite that far, walking, and it seems less with a few good drams under your belt. I crossed the street and took the track that brings you out on the Cupar road. The neighbours had been and gone before I got home, but one of them brought the wife over to fetch the Land-Rover later in the day, I wasna' fit to drive.'

He fell silent again, sipping at the soup which was still too hot to drink.

'It shouldn't be difficult to prove that your Land-Rover was in the pub car park all night,' Beth said. 'How many cars were there when you came out?'

'Damned if I know. I never went round the back to look. But I'd parked in the furthest bit, beyond the wee stand of trees. It's a thin chance that somebody'd notice it there. And there was precious few cars in the car park when I left it. Folk have more sense than to take a car out at Hogmanay. I wish to God I'd been one of them.'

'They wouldn't be harassing you,' Isobel said, looking up from her papers, 'unless they had some hard evidence.'

'Aye. I just can't make sense o't,' Angus said miserably. 'There was blood and hair on my front bumper. They showed it to me and asked me to explain it. I said I'd not an idea in my head how it could have got there.'

'Just on the bumper?' Beth asked. 'Not on the bonnet?'

'Just the bumper. But I'd washed the damned thing when the wife got back wi't, just for something to do until I was sober and to keep the de Forgan kids out of the wife's hair. Damned if I ken how I missed the bumper,' Angus said frankly, 'except I was still stotting. The fact I washed it at all looks bad to them.'

'It would,' Isobel said. 'Could somebody else have driven it away, run the man down, and put it back?'

'I canna' think it. It was just exactly where I'd left it and parked in the same gear – the handbrake doesn't work worth a damn. A Land-Rover's easy enough to break intil, they can be hot-wired and there's no steering lock, not on that model. There was no sign of interference, naethin' like that at all. There's even been a wee drip of oil from the sump plug this past week and when I went to take a look on the way here there was just the one small stain to be seen. They'd've been two if anybody'd driven it and put it back, me or anybody else.'

'You told the police that?' I asked.

'Aye. They think I drove it mysel' an' put it back there to give mysel' a sort of an alias.'

'Alibi,' I said.

'That's what I was meaning,' he snapped with a touch of his old fire. But the spark died away immediately. 'There's a whole lot more. I couldna' make head nor tail of some of their questions, but they were asking – and in front of my wife – if I'd not had a fancy woman in Dundee. And then they got on to me about yon tearaway that was killed a few years back.'

'The one mentioned in the local paper?' I asked. 'The biker?'

'That's the one.'

'I thought that that was only a bit of wild guesswork by the reporters.'

'Seemingly not. Or else the police are making the same guesses. I'd had a run-in wi' the skellum myself and it was all on the record, the way it worked out. I was keepering for old Mr Crae – he's dead now, rest his soul – and that lad, McKendrick his name was, he was a member of a motorbike gang, the worst sort, all black leather and nastiness. He used to come onto the land and tear around on his bike, scaring the birds right over the boundaries and knocking over the feeders. Sometimes he'd be with others but more often alone. Rode right at me once and near bowled me over.

'Left to myself I'd've knocked him off his bike and sorted him out with a whippy stick, but Mr Crae said not to put mysel' in the wrong. So we did it by the book, took him to court to ask for an interdict restraining him from coming on the land, and I was the main witness. But he denied it a' and swore blind that I'd attacked him when he'd only stopped at the roadside near by to fix his chain. The sheriff didn't see through him and we lost out.

'Not long after, he was killed. I'd nothing to do wi't. I was questioned four times, but there was no evidence either way. I'm thinking they'd have made a case if they could but the Fiscal's office wasn't for it.'

'It was before we moved here,' Beth said. 'What really happened?'

Isobel, her nose still in her papers, made a sound of disgust.

Angus shook his head sadly. 'It was a terrible business. I'd wanted him to get his comeuppance, but I wouldna' wish what happened on the devil himself, not even on Saddam Hussein. Somebody took a hammer to him. But it was nothing as merciful as a knock on the head. Both his knees were broken and his hands were mashed. Then his mouth was taped up and he was dumped not far from here in Tentsmuir Forest and left to die of exposure. He couldna' crawl and he couldna' pull away the tape so he just lay there and died.'

Angus buried his face in his soup mug as though to wash away a bad taste. The room was silent except for the rustle as Isobel gathered up her papers. As a local, she had heard the details before. Beth and I were struck dumb by the raw cruelty of it. Angus might have a temper but I knew that he could never have left a man to die. In the Falklands, I had seen him carry a wounded prisoner to safety although he was bleeding from a bullet wound inflicted earlier by the same man after waving a white flag of surrender.

Beth refilled Angus's mug with soup. He looked down without seeming to notice it. 'You'll see why I need to get my affairs straight,' he said. 'I've done nothing wrong

53

and I'm not afraid of the law, but if they charge me wi' anything more than leaving the scene of an accident I could be . . . busy . . . for a good while. I'm trying to fix for somebody to look after the business if the worst comes to the worst. One thing I'll need to know soon is, are you interested in my proposition?'

I pulled my mind back from death and thought about Angus's proposal. As both he and Isobel had implied, it made a great deal of sense for a training kennels to be closely associated with a shoot. My subconscious mind, I discovered, had thrown up a dozen ways in which any extra work could be absorbed into our daily routine. We would have to borrow, but if the proposition was sound – which had yet to be established although the figures that Angus had written down looked good – it would be into the black by the end of the first year. My reluctance, I realized, came from a deep disquiet about attitudes.

During my boyhood, the owner of land might shoot over it with friends or guests. Economic pressure had diminished that gentlemanly scene almost to vanishing point. We had seen instead the rise of the syndicate, paying a rent for the sporting rights, sharing the costs or the labour of keepering, continuing to make improvements to the woods and coverts and learning all the time about how to hold the game and how best to walk up or drive the land. This I could understand and approve.

I was less happy about the new growth of commercial sporting estates, letting the shooting by the day or week and charging by the number of birds in the bag. For the busy visitor, it might make a sort of sense. He was relieved of the distractions of operating a syndicate. The cost of getting his few days of top-class shooting might not be much greater than the subscription to a syndicate of equal quality, on top of which he could choose his days and shoot in a different part of the country every weekend, if he so wished and if his purse was deep enough. But somehow I felt that he would have made a bad bargain. The changing scenery might please his eye but he would never come to identify himself with the fields and coverts.

Beth and Isobel were watching me. I decided that if the better-heeled shooting men were pleased to put money our way in exchange for only superficial enjoyment, it would be only gracious to accept it with equal pleasure.

'We could be,' I said at last. 'We'd have to think it over after we knew exactly what land you were talking about.'

Angus, it was clear, was still afraid of being outbid. 'You wouldn't—'

'We'd need you as much as you'd need us,' I said.

He thought it over, nodding slowly, and then shrugged. 'Foleyknowe,' he said. 'Between the Carse of Gowrie and the Pentland Hills. Not too far from here, going over the Road Bridge.'

'But it's as bare as your hand,' Beth said.

Angus shook his head and managed a half smile. 'It looks that way,' he said. 'That's why there's no interest. But Mr Crae, when he was alive and had the sporting lease, put in more than three thousand trees, mixed deciduous and conifers. You don't see them. For one thing, they're only three years old, just ready for a burst of growth. For another, they're mostly along the streams down in the low ground, out of the sight of the passers-by. His idea was that you put game crops and feeders higher up. Then you're driving the birds off the high ground towards home in the woods. That way they should be high and fast.'

Isobel and Beth were still watching me, waiting for my judgement.

'I'll go over and take a look within the next few days,' I said. 'Then we'll let you know.'

'That'll have to do.' Angus looked at the clock on the mantelpiece and heaved himself to his feet. 'Now I must away for home.'

'If you've no other calls to make around here,' I said, 'one of us will give you a lift.'

FOUR

Beth had a profound distrust of any man exuding such a macho image as did Angus, but she was always sympathetic towards anyone in trouble. She invited him to stay for a bite of lunch, but Angus, now that he had said his piece, was in a hurry to go.

When I offered Angus a lift home, I had had Daffy in mind as chauffeur – her eccentricities did not extend to her driving. But the usual female conspiracy went into action to keep me from standing around in the cold or tiring myself out and I found myself elected as driver.

We loaded Angus's bike into the back of my old estate car and set off.

'When you first parked behind the inn,' I said, 'were any other Land-Rovers there already?'

He racked his memory for a full minute before replying. 'There was maybe one,' he said at last. 'Or maybe it was a Fourtrack. If there was, it needn't mean anything. Every farmer has one similar. And half the shooting men, if they can't afford a Range Rover or a Shogun. The other half have a family car and something smaller like a Suzuki, or else the family car's a four-wheel drive. Anyway, I couldn't be sure. I wasn't looking out for Land-Rovers, I was watching for the Jag of the man I was to meet, in case he'd arrived before me.'

'Did you recognize even a single car?' I asked. 'Or did you meet anyone in the bar who couldn't have walked there? If so, you'd have a starting point. One man might recognize another car when he came or left and so onward. It's the kind of information your solicitor will need if the case comes to court.'

'I thought of that for myself,' he said. 'There was maybe a dozen cars but I wasn't looking at them. The only man I could swear to was one I saw inside. Willy Chambers.'

'I don't know him,' I said.

'No, you wouldn't. He lives a mile or two from me, in one of those new bungalows with as much character as a paper bag. Drives around in a flashy Mercedes.'

'You didn't see the Mercedes in the car park?'

'Not to notice it. I've been to see him, but it's no go. He hates my guts. See, he's one of these smiling characters who aye gets his own way. Whatever it is, he does it first and apologizes afterwards and charms his way out of it. He aye stops just short of the point where it's worth anyone's while to take him to court.' Angus seemed more comfortable now that we had moved away from his problems to where he could be his usual abrasive self. 'He wanted to build a cluster of upmarket houses on the rough land just behind my place and I wasn't for it. But he made a start before his planning permission was through, on the say-so of one of the councillors. So I made a song and dance about it and he was stopped. That made them come and take a right look at it and they could see that it was in the wrong place. What's more,' Angus added with satisfaction, 'I got onto the Nature Conservancy Council and all those chiels, and now it's designated a Site of Special Scientific Interest.'

'And he's stuck with the cost of the land and a penalty for breaking his contract with the builder.'

'Plus a backhander to the councillor, I wouldn't doubt. I spoke to him, but what he told me was a load of shit. He'd like fine to me get shafted.' Angus stopped dead and lowered his voice. 'I was wondering . . .'

'Yes?'

'I swear to God that I know nothing about any of this,' he burst out. 'Do you think . . . Captain

57

Cunningham . . . you could help me? Even if it's only advice? I've nobody I could bring myself even to talk it over wi'. I've a cousin near here, he's in the police, but he's no good to me. He's been told his job's on the line if he as much as speaks to me.'

I let the word 'Captain' go by for once. Angus was appealing to me as soldier to officer. I realized that responsibility for one's men was a burden that never lifted. It was a one-sided obligation but it was there nevertheless.

I had no desire to embroil myself in Angus Todd's affairs. Despite my assessment of his character, I knew that such judgements could often be wrong. Angus might be as guilty as hell and I might seem guilty by association. But he had served me well and I owed him my help. 'You can come and talk it over any time,' I told him. 'And if I get the chance I'll see what I can find out.'

I turned off the tarmac road onto a gravel track leading to where Angus's house, formed by the neat conversion of two old workmen's cottages, stood against a background of sheds and rearing pens. The place looked naked without the Land-Rover at the door. 'My best advice,' I added, 'would be to get a really good solicitor on the case as soon as possible.'

'That'll cost,' he said gloomily.

'It'll cost a damn sight more if the thing goes the whole way and you have to face a charge of murder.'

There was just enough room to turn a vehicle. I backed round and stopped. A boy and girl were playing with Angus's retriever on a patch of grass but Bruce, his black cocker spaniel, ran to the car and jumped up against the passenger door.

'Bruce hasn't been out at stud, has he?' I asked. Guilty or innocent, if Angus had accepted the pick of a litter instead of a stud fee, he might well be reluctant to admit to the lost pup.

He knew what I was driving at. 'Just the once,' he said. 'To a bitch in St Andrews. And not an all black pup in the litter. Get down, you bugger,' he added to Bruce.

We got out of the car. As Angus lifted the bike out of the back, Mrs Todd came to the door in a clean apron, a homely woman in middle age but with delicate features that could still look unexpectedly girlish when the light and the mood were right. She looked a question at Angus and he nodded. 'The Captain says that he'll help,' he said. He wheeled the bicycle towards a small shed.

She smiled unhappily and came forward, offering her hand for a shake. 'I'll do what I can,' I said. 'It may not be much.'

I tried to detach my hand but she held onto it tightly. 'It'll mean a lot to him, just to have somebody on his side that he can trust.' She had her voice back under control although I preferred her natural voice, accent and dialect and all, to the rather prissy diction that she used when she was 'talking pan loaf'. 'He hasn't many friends around here. It's not everybody who can stand up against the sharp side of his tongue.' She sounded almost proud of Angus's gift of invective. 'Won't you come in?'

'Another time. My lunch will be on the table,' I said.

She nodded sombre acceptance and then brightened as the laughter of the two children reached us. 'Mrs de Forgan leaves the children here when she's over this way,' she said. 'I've known them since they were toddlers.'

I recovered my hand and got back into the car. She stooped to the window, effectively preventing me from either getting out again or driving off. I wound down the glass.

'Angus would do none of those things,' she said. 'I know him. He has a temper, but if he did violence to another man it would be fair and face to face. And as for his having a fancy woman in Dundee, that's just haivering. He couldn't have kept such a thing a secret from me. He's a once a week man, regular as clockwork, and always has been ever since we were courting. There's been no change in that department.'

She stood up and stepped back. I drove away before any more confidences could be wished on me.

*

59

When I got back to the Three Oaks, Isobel had embarked on her weekly check of our stock for infections, ticks, and wounds while Daffy was busy with the eternal chores of cleaning, feeding, and exercising. Beth was alone in the house. She put some lunch on the table and stood over me to make sure that I ate it.

'Angus asked me to help him,' I told her between mouthfuls.

'To prove his innocence?'

'I suppose so. Or at least to throw doubt on his guilt.'

'Suppose that he's guilty?' she asked, putting her finger, as usual, on my worst fears.

'In that case I'll have wasted my time, that's all. A search for the truth can't do any actual harm.'

'Some of the dirt could rub off on you.'

'I'm not sure that I care a lot for the opinion of anybody dim enough to think that way,' I said.

'Even clients?'

'I'll just have to risk it. I owe Angus that much. And I don't think he's guilty.'

'I don't have much of an opinion either way,' she said thoughtfully. 'It doesn't look too good. But it would be awful if he was perfectly innocent but nobody was prepared to stand by him.' She settled in the chair opposite mine. 'All right. I'll help if I can. Don't go tearing around all over the place, tiring yourself out and missing meals. Where do we start?'

I gave it some thought. 'The easiest starting point, and one where we have an edge over the police, is the pups. We know who to speak to and what to say. There can't have been so many litters of black working cockers in mid-November and, of those, many of the pups will still be with their dams. We could find out which pups can't be accounted for.'

Beth was quick to pounce on what she saw as an opportunity to keep me at rest in front of a warm fire. 'You could get on with that now,' she said.

'Later. More people are at home in the evenings,' I

said. I have a phobia about running up phone-bills. At least the calls would be cheaper in the evening. 'And with the championship coming up, our two hopefuls need to be kept up to scratch.'

'Do you need me to come and fire the dummy-launcher for you?'

'What about Sam?'

'I could bring him along in the papoose-thing. He'll only sleep all afternoon anyway.'

'Not if you're shooting off the dummy-launcher,' I pointed out.

'That's true. Well, all right. Wrap up well.'

I wrapped up well, fetched a gun, a blank cartridge adaptor, some blanks, and a belt of shot-gun cartridges from my store, slung a bag of dummies and the dummy-launcher over my shoulder, and went to collect the two spaniels. I took them across the road at heel and then let them blow off steam, racing each other in circles as we crossed a vacant pasture to the Moss. I soon decided that I had wrapped up rather too well for carrying a load of equipment over uneven going.

I could hear shots from the Moss, which boded ill for steadiness training. The Moss was riddled with holes and all the rabbits would by now be underground. The prospect of having exclusive access to a commercial shoot made more and more sense. We would be able to start the season with the dogs knowing the difference between the scents of a pheasant and a songbird. Well, I could still do some work with the dummies, but first I ought to make contact with the shooters and let them know that I was around with the dogs.

I cast Rowan out and he hunted through the scattered gorse within gunshot of me but, as I thought, any rabbits were well underground. I called him back to heel and we pushed through the last stand of alders.

Near the middle of the Moss, on the one flat and dry stretch of ground, two men had set up a light clay pigeon trap and were having a little informal practice. As I approached, the one with the over-under gun in his hands dropped his barrels and I did the same.

The other man got up from his seat on the clay trap. 'Sorry if we've spoiled things for you,' he said. I recognized Constable Peel who was, I knew, a clay pigeon enthusiast.

'One door shuts, another opens,' I said. 'It gives me a chance to remind the dogs that they stay put until they're sent out. Do you mind if I join you?'

'You're more than welcome.' His Irish accent was more noticeable when he was off duty. 'Do you know Harry Piat?'

I shook hands with Harry Piat, a small, lean man with a face that looked ready to smile. I had seen him somewhere before.

They changed places. The dogs sat as though they had taken root while Piat missed two curling clays and broke seven, so I took a turn. Rowan ruined my concentration. He had developed a weird habit of shaking his head and snorting whenever I missed. Both dogs stirred in sudden interest when I exchanged my gun for the dummy-launcher. Giving them each a long retrieve, with a stop whistle during the outrun, interrupted the claybusting for a minute or two, but I made up for it by taking over the trap for a while.

'I must be going,' Harry Piat said suddenly. 'Got to get ready for the night shift. Do you want anything lugged back to your house?'

'I can manage,' Peel said. 'Thanks anyway.'

Piat shook hands with me again, patted both dogs and set off across the Moss.

'Another policeman?' I asked.

Peel shook his head. 'Not him. He lives in Wormit but works in Dundee. NCR, I think. We're members of the same clay club.'

'I've seen him before.' It was coming back to me. 'He was in the bar at Hogmanay.'

'We knew that.' Peel looked at me thoughtfully and

decided to open up a bit more. 'He couldn't tell us any-thing useful. His wife had to ask a neighbour for a lift over here so that she could drive him home. At least he still had the sense to phone for her.'

He was practising for an imminent competition. I threw some more clays for him and he returned the compliment by using the dummy-launcher before we decided to quit.

'I'll pick up the unbroken clays,' Peel said. 'They cost money. No need for you to wait around.'

'The dogs can make short work of it,' I said. 'They've done the job before.'

The trap had remained in the one place with the shoot-ers moving around to get a change of birds, so that the unbroken clays were scattered over a small area. The two spaniels galloped happily around, retrieving the clay pigeons in their gentle mouths.

It struck me as unusual that a policeman involved in a serious case should be at leisure during the working week. 'You're taking your day off, I suppose,' I said.

'That's right. I'm back on routine duties now.'

In my experience, officers on a major enquiry usually stayed with it. I must have shown some surprise because he said, 'There were reasons.'

'Angus Todd being your cousin?'

It was his turn to show surprise. 'You know that, do you?'

'He asked me for help.'

'I can understand that, you having been his officer in the Falklands. He often talks about those days. Army life must have suited him. He says that he's getting soft now.'

The dogs were hunting in vain, pausing hopefully to bring us a piece of broken clay pigeon now and again. I hoped that none of the championship ground had ever been used for clay pigeon shooting – Isobel's face would be red if she sent one of the dogs for a game bird and it came back with an orange midi. Peel swung the trap onto his shoulder and picked up the bag of clay pigeons.

'At least it's lighter going back,' he said. I took his gun

and we set off. 'As soon as the big bugs saw that Angus was going to come under suspicion and when it dawned on them that I was related to him, I was off the case in two minutes flat,' he said. 'They told me not to go near him again.'

'Did anybody tell you not to go near me?'

'No,' he said slowly. 'They didn't.'

We came to a favourite resting place of mine, a fallen tree beside the small pond. Lob went for a quick paddle, to cool off after the hard work. By tacit agreement, we settled there. I had been glad to move but now I was glad to rest again. Waxproofed cotton makes an excellent waterproof coat but it does tend to keep the sweat in while letting the body's warmth escape. Peel gave a grunt of relief.

'Do you think your cousin's guilty?' I asked.

He made a noise that could have passed for a laugh but was utterly without amusement. 'Guilty of what? He's only charged with hit-and-run at the moment. I think he's capable of knocking down a pedestrian and driving off in a moment of panic. That's probably true of most of us, given the right circumstances. The cases I've seen . . . The very last people you'd expect. The evidence on his Land-Rover seems cast iron.'

'They've matched the hairs to the dead man?'

He nodded soberly. 'But to make it into murder they have to link it with one or both of the Dundee killings, and that I could not believe. Angus has a temper but there's no cruelty in him. More than once I've seen him stop the car to knock an injured rabbit on the head. When we were boys, he found some stranded tadpoles after a tank was emptied. He tried to give them the kiss of life. You don't get more compassionate than that.'

That agreed with my own opinion. Angus had fought with dedication and cunning but I had seen him use his field dressing on his wounded prisoner while his own wound was dripping blood. 'Let's stay with the evidence,' I said. 'Were there no traces on the bonnet of the Land-Rover?'

He glanced at me and then looked away, across the pond to the low hills in the distance. 'You'll never let on that I told you anything?'

'Definitely not,' I said.

'I shouldn't be talking. But I can't think of any other way to help Angus. I don't know it all, of course. I was a pair of feet, a mouth and ears, fit to ask a hundred people the same questions but not to think about the answers, just to bring them back and deliver to hand, just like those spaniels of yours. But inevitably I was sometimes around when the brains discussed the case between them.

'The Land-Rover's bonnet was clean and undamaged. That worries them. The damage to the dead man suggested that his head and hands must have come down on the bonnet and there was green cellulose paint impacted on them. Of course, Angus admits he washed the vehicle.'

'And missed the bumper? That seems unlikely?'

'He was still half-cut. All the same, Angus has one of those power hoses. Damn nearly rolls a car over. I was wondering myself how he could soap and hose the Land-Rover, leaving hairs as well as blood on the bumper. And a Land-Rover's bodywork may be solid but you'd expect more than the bumper to show signs of a smack like that.'

'Did they send the bumper away for testing?' I asked. 'Or did they examine the whole vehicle in one piece? Or don't you know?'

Constable Peel blinked at me for some seconds before I saw the penny drop. 'Oho! So that's the way your mind's working! No, there was a forensic science team of three men borrowed from Edinburgh. It was my job to fetch them from the station, and later to show them the Land-Rover in the police garage and to stand around in case they wanted their noses wiped or coffee fetched. They lifted the hairs and then took away swabs from all over the vehicle. You reckon somebody might have swapped bumpers?'

'It crossed my mind,' I said.

He thought about it and then shook his head doubtfully. 'Not an easy job. It was dark where the Land-Rover was parked.'

'Suppose he drove on after the accident,' I said.

'Accident?'

'Fatality, then. Suppose he slacked off the bolts on his own bumper somewhere near a lamp, or even took it right off. And then came back just before dawn, while the rest of us were all sleeping it off. He'd have it fresh in his mind just where the bolts were placed and what tools he needed.'

'That still wouldn't explain how Angus came to miss the bumper when he washed the rest of it,' he said, frowning.

'No. But it's a start. Leave it for now. What about the coat the dead man was wearing? Would it have fitted Angus?'

He shrugged. 'It was an M size. I wasn't there when they questioned him, but I know for a fact that Angus has half a dozen coats, waxproof and Goretex and I don't know what-all. Mr Crae was always buying them, looking for the perfect shooting coat, something dry and windproof that wouldn't hinder his arms when he was swinging a gun, and he used to pass on to Angus the ones he didn't like.'

'But there was nothing to link it positively with Angus?'

'Not that I know of. But I do know that they found black dog-hairs in the right-hand pocket. From a small dog, and probably a young one they thought, but they couldn't say for sure.' He turned his head to look around, as though he suspected listening ears among the straggling trees. 'My guess is that if Angus was brought to trial now, they could get convictions for dangerous driving, manslaughter, leaving the scene, I don't know what-all. But not murder. Not yet. If they spend the next few weeks looking for evidence that will count against him and not looking for anything that goes in his favour, who knows?'

The digression had given me time to begin sorting my still disordered thoughts. A breeze had sprung up and I was feeling the cold, but I might never find Peel in such a confiding mood again. 'What did you find out about the people in the bar that night?'

'Not a damn thing of any use. They came and went. Some of them noticed others, most didn't. One couple had a Land-Rover registered to them, but they came in the family car and their son was in Dundee with the Land-Rover.'

'And in the car park?'

'A slow build-up to a peak about ten p.m. and then thinning out again. One man, just one, thought that he remembered another Land-Rover parked near the back door late on, but it could have been a Shogun, a Nissan Patrol, Dacia Duster, or a Fourtrack. Any damn jeep, in fact, from a Suzuki to a Range Rover.'

I was getting answers without getting anything else. Except cold. The light was beginning to go and the dogs were restless. But there was one more urgent question. 'Was Angus asked who he was meeting? I forgot to ask him.'

'He was asked all right,' Peel said grimly. 'But not a word would he say. When he was pressed, that's when he blew up and refused to say any more about anything. Two of the bar staff saw him speaking with a man when it was nearly midnight, about the time Dinnet left, but their descriptions only fit where they touch. They could be describing two different men.' He peered at his watch in the fading light. 'It's time I was moving. We can talk again.'

We got to our feet and shouldered our burdens.

The prolonged infection which had (as I could now admit to myself) nearly carried me off had left me seriously underweight and very vulnerable to chills. But I never learned. Sitting with Constable Peel on the fallen tree in deepening dusk, I had felt and ignored the warning signs.

The two spaniels had been away from home at the routine time for the evening meal. I kennelled them, reminded Daffy to dry and feed them, and found Henry, Isobel, and Beth already embarked on the customary winding-down session in the sitting room. Sam was also present in body but soundly asleep in his Carricot. I could feel the deep shivers, the crawling skin and the imminence of cold sweats which meant that I had overtaxed myself again, but I was determined not to let the others see that I was off colour. Perhaps this time the symptoms might not progress. I took a whisky instead of my usual beer and moved one of the wing-chairs closer to the fire.

Scribbled papers were scattered among the glasses on the low table. This was a normal state for the room, but it was too early to be discussing next season's competition entries and the notes looked too random to be Isobel's proposals for breeding policy. They seemed to be lists of names and phone numbers, in several handwritings, most of them followed by ticks or short comments.

Beth saw me craning my neck. 'We've been tracking down cocker pups,' she said.

The cheap rate had not started – but our drinks, I reminded myself, would have cost more than the phone-calls. 'Any luck?' I asked.

'Not a lot,' said Isobel.

'It's too soon to try Kennel Club registrations,' Beth said, 'even if we could be sure that they were all going to be registered. We tried known breeders and the gun dog clubs and carried on from there, working outwards from the nearest ones. Of course, we couldn't be sure about amateur breeders with a family bitch, but Isobel's been calling her fellow vets and getting one or two names.'

'We've covered most of Central Scotland,' Henry said, 'and found five litters so far born around the right time, but most of the black pups are accounted for. Several numbers aren't answering.'

'I'll try them again this evening,' Beth said. 'How did you get on?'

'They're both as ready as they ever will be.' I looked at Isobel. We tried to be as flexible as we could be, exchanging jobs to suit circumstances; but, in general, the rough work was left to Daffy, Beth could do any job around the place, I was the trainer while Isobel kept the books and records and looked after the dogs' health. But, in addition, Isobel had surprised all of us including herself by turning into a great handler in competitions. She had an unflappable temperament and an uncanny instinct for whatever a dog or a bird would do next.

'Rowan's still inclined to be impetuous,' I told her. 'We'd better find somewhere near the ground and get him out there really early to blow off steam on the first morning. And the second, if he's still in the running. He usually settles down after a few minutes. Be ready with the stop whistle and give a quick peep if he looks in the least like running in. The judge may dock you a mark, but that's better than being put out for unsteadiness.'

Isobel nodded and I could see that she was filing away the information and the suggestion somewhere in the intricate philosophy that lay behind her success. 'It's something from his early training,' she said. 'Thank God he never passes it on genetically!'

'You were late coming back,' Beth said. She was watching me closely, sensing something wrong. As much to distract her as for any other reason, I told them in detail of what I had learned from Constable Peel. I made the story as short as I could. My voice was becoming hoarse.

Henry got up and refilled glasses. My job usually, but my legs were trembling. 'Interesting,' Henry said. 'From the rather obscured viewpoint that we had at the time, I thought that the vehicle caught him on the legs and lower body, as you'd expect. It threw him forward and hit him again as he went down. The Constable was right in what he said – you'd expect plenty of signs on the bonnet. Not just blood and hair but dents. Land-Rovers are solidly built, but not . . .' He glanced in Beth's direction and came to a halt.

69

'Not to take a skull coming down hard,' Beth said. 'It's all right, Henry, I'd already thought of that for myself. I shan't get the collywobbles if we talk about it.'

'Most middle-aged Land-Rovers are all over dents anyway,' Isobel said.

'Not Angus's,' said Beth. 'He kept his like new.'

She was still watching me. With the Spaniel Championships almost upon us, the last thing I wanted was to be laid up with Beth as my nurse-cum-warder. I tried to hide the signs but when I relaxed my jaw my teeth chattered audibly.

'That does it,' Beth said. She jumped up and felt my forehead. 'You've been out in the cold too long again. Hot bath and into bed for you.'

'Not yet,' I protested. 'I've got to see Angus again. There are more questions—'

Beth stood up, got hold of my arm and pulled with surprising strength. 'Definitely not!' she said.

'You're on a loser, John.' Isobel was looking anxious but at the same time amused. 'Give in, or you won't be fit for the championship.'

I would have put up more resistance but my head was beginning to swim. I let Beth drag me to my feet. 'Somebody fetch Angus over to see me tomorrow,' I croaked.

Beth hauled me upstairs and ran a hot bath for me. The delicious heat seeped into me and yet I was still cold. As I knew from experience, it was possible to be hot on the outside and remain chilled deep within, like a badly thawed joint of beef. While I soaked, Beth fed me with the various pills that the doctor had left for such contingencies – an antibiotic to keep infection off my lungs, something to take the fever down, and God knows what else.

Beth had a hot towel and warm pyjamas ready and the electric blanket was on. There must have been a sleeping pill somewhere among the others. I was hardly between the sheets before the world faded away.

FIVE

I woke slowly. My pyjamas were moist with sweat, but the fever had abated and although I was light-headed my mind was clear. I could hear the usual noises of the house and kennels. They were not early morning noises. About nine thirty, I guessed, and when I opened my eyes and looked at the clock I was only a few minutes out.

Somebody opened the door, looked in, and went away again. I was too late to see who it was but they must have seen that I was surfacing because a few minutes later the door was bumped open and Daffy came in with a tray. She was wearing Wellingtons and jeans, but the workmanlike effect was spoiled by a frilly blouse which might once have been the top section of a ball-gown. Her hair had reverted to what I thought was probably its natural colour but stood up in spikes and her lipstick was orange with green eyeshadow.

'Sit up for a moment,' she said, 'while I rearrange the pillows.'

'Damn that for a lark,' I retorted. 'I'm getting up. Find me some clothes.'

Her hair had given her a look of terror until she laughed at me. 'Not a hope,' she said, setting down the tray. 'Put it out of your mind.'

'Who's the boss around here?'

'That's a moot point.' She snickered suddenly. 'If you have to ask the question, who am I to answer it? I've seen you before, remember, after one of your bouts.' She looked at me consideringly, enjoying her moment of power. 'I'll tell you what I'll do. If you can get out of bed on your own and stand still with your eyes closed for ten seconds, I'll fetch your clothes.'

When I tried to sit up my head began to swim again. Daffy propped me up and put the tray on my knees. Cereal, toast, a boiled egg and tea. 'Where's Beth?' I asked.

'Out. Taking Sam and some pups up the fields. If you've had breakfast before she gets back I'm to hump you through to the bathroom. Your clean pyjamas are on the towel rail.'

'You're both dreaming,' I said with my mouth full. I had missed my evening meal and the food tasted marvellous.

'Otherwise, I'm to give you a blanket bath.'

The idea of being given a blanket bath by somebody who looked like Daffy was daunting. I finished my breakfast while she ran a bath and then leaned on her as far as the bathroom. My muscles seemed to have turned into spaghetti.

At the bathroom door, I stopped. 'This is as far as you come.'

'You'll never make it on your own.'

'Go away,' I said.

'I don't know what you're worrying about,' she said. 'If you've got something I haven't seen ten of before, don't be a spoilsport.'

I shut the door against her and managed to strip without falling over. I heard her start down the stairs, singing to the tune of 'The green, green grass of home'. '*I open the door,*' she sang, '*and here comes Mary, teeth of gold and lips all hairy . . .* '

I lowered myself carefully into the hot water. My mind, still erratic, teased at the words. Lips of gold and . . . No, that still wasn't right. Hair of gold and teeth . . . No. Lips like cherries. That was it. Now I could relax.

Ten minutes later, clean and refreshed and feeling a little steadier, I tottered back to the bedroom. Daffy had just finished making up the bed with clean sheets.

'I am going downstairs,' I said.

'Mrs Cunningham said that you'd say that. She told me to push you into the bed and sit on you until she gets back. She says she's spoken to Mr Todd and he's coming to see you. Until then, you can twiddle your thumbs or anything else you want to twiddle.'

I flopped down on the bed. 'Did Beth really say that last bit?' I asked.

Daffy grinned. 'Twiddling? No, that was all my own.'

I lay back and she tucked me in, quite gently by her standards. 'All the same,' I said, 'I'll have to get up and about soon if I'm going to drive Mrs Kitts to the championships.'

Our logistics would have been greatly simplified if Isobel had driven herself to and from field trials. This she was perfectly willing to do, but we conspired to prevent it just as the others conspired to keep me warm and dry. Isobel was an occasional drinker and in the letdown after the concentration of handling in competition it took only the euphoria of a good result or the despair of a bad one to set her off. Henry, as well as being past the age for driving long distances, was little better. Since Sam had appeared on the horizon, Beth was no longer available. Daffy had only passed her driving test a few weeks earlier. She managed well on the local roads; whether she was ready for a long drive on motorways was another matter. But when needs must, the devil, or somebody who looks remarkably like him, may drive . . .

'You'll have to go,' I said.

'All the way to North Wales? Don't be daft. Who'd do the heavy work here? Anyway,' Daffy said, 'it's all arranged. Mr Kitts is going along for the ride and Rex is going to drive them.'

'Rex?' I had not intended to sound so surprised, but I had never associated Rex with any useful activity.

'He's a good driver,' Daffy said indignantly, 'and at least he can stay sober when he wants to.'

'But he hasn't driven my car before.'

'He has, you know,' Daffy said and she went away, leaving me with another worry. Had Rex and Daffy been borrowing the car when my back was turned? What kind of antics had been performed in the spacious back of it? Well, I decided, I could overlook it just as long as they had parked with discretion. I would hate to think that the neighbours had recognized the car, seen a bobbing behind, and mistaken it for mine.

Beth returned and paid me a visit, careful to hide her anxiety. ('That girl,' I said, 'will have to go,' but she only laughed.) The doctor came, examined me, and repeated all the advice, about putting on some weight and keeping warm, that I had already demonstrated to be impractical.

Not long after the doctor's departure, I heard a heavier vehicle arrive and Beth brought Angus Todd up to see me. He sat down nervously on the edge of the bedroom chair. To do him justice, he seemed more concerned on my behalf than his own.

'It's happened before,' I said, 'and I dare say it'll happen again. It takes it out of me, but it's only the aftermath of that bug I picked up in Central America. At least I get over it each time a little quicker than the time before. Do I gather that the police have let you have your Land-Rover back? Or is it a borrow?'

'It's mine,' he said.

'Did they make any comment when they returned it?'

'Just that it seemed to be running rich. The bobby that brought it back didn't know anything about the case, or said he didn't, but he's got it running better.'

Angus spoke listlessly. Something was missing. Not just his usual aggressive humour but something deeper. My guess was that, confronted by proof of what he knew to be untrue, the reasoning part of his mind was stunned into inactivity. The best help that I could give him would be to get him thinking again.

'You swear that you didn't drive again at Hogmanay?'

'On my mother's grave,' he said, without seeming to care. The fact that his mother was still alive and living in

74

sheltered housing in Cupar robbed the oath of much of its value.

'You weren't so pissed that you could have driven and forgotten about it?'

'I was fu', but not that fu'.'

'Then what do you think happened?'

He shrugged and then made an effort. 'I can't believe someone else drove it. The best I can think is that somebody with another Land-Rover knocked the man down and then smeared blood and hair onto my bumper, but I'm damned if I see how he could do it so that it looked natural enough to fool the Forensic lads. They showed me the marks and they looked just the way they would.'

'Do us both a favour,' I said. 'Go down and look at your Land-Rover. Take a good look at the front bumper. Then come back and tell me two things. One, is that the bumper that was on it last year? And, two, do the bolts show any sign of having been tampered with?' He looked puzzled. I went on, 'You must know what I mean. Nuts and washers never go back exactly in the same place and spanners leave marks in the paint. Take a look and see if there's any undercoat or bright metal showing.'

It was as though I had given him a start with jump-leads. I could almost see his mind spin, catch, and begin to tick over. He jumped to his feet. 'By Christ!' he said.

In two minutes he was back. This time he sat comfortably in the chair, worried still but much less tense. His expression, partly obscured by whiskers, was difficult to read but I thought that I could detect the first faint dawning of hope. 'I'm damned if I can be sure,' he said. 'The bumper's like mine. Well, it would be. It's about the same age with the right amount of dents and a wee bit of rust. But whether it's the same one . . . I never really looked at the bloody thing. That vehicle's just a gadget for hauling me from place to place. I keep it clean because I wouldn't want folk to see it any other way – that's your army bullshit coming out again,' he added with a flash of his old spirit, 'but as long as it goes, who needs to look at it? I have a feeling it's not the same, or am I kidding myself? I mind one time in the old days when yon daft bugger McHenry swapped rifles with me. There was nothing different about his one, we had to check the numbers to be sure, but it just didn't look right to me.'

'And the bolts?'

'Again, I couldn't swear to it. There are marks – they're a wee bit rusted, but the roads have been salted these last few days. It doesn't take long for rust to form on bare metal when there's salt around.' He frowned. 'Wouldn't the Forensics lads have noticed anything unusual?'

'I don't suppose that many of the bolts are still exactly where Rover bolted them on, umpteen years ago. When was your bumper last taken off?' I asked him.

'I don't know that it's ever been off. Unless when they put in a new radiator three years back . . .'

'Ask them. And what you've got to do, the minute you leave here, is take it to a mechanical engineer, somebody whose qualifications would impress a court. The main agent for Land-Rovers might do. Have him look at it first and then he must undo the bolts and give a written opinion as to whether the bumper had been off recently.'

'I'll do that, of course,' Angus said. 'If he says yes . . .'

'You'll still not be out of the wood as far as a court is concerned,' I said. 'You could have had time to take it off and put it back yourself, to mislead them – if they think you're bright enough to have thought of that for yourself, which I doubt.'

'At least I'm not so daft I'd sit around in a cold wind getting my bum frozen off when I'm not fit,' he retorted.

'*Touché*. But at least it would show that there is another possible explanation. If it comes to court, tell your lawyers that they must get the police to testify, before your witness is produced, that the bumper wasn't removed for scientific testing.'

Angus was nodding. 'Got you,' he said. 'What else?'

'And if you've any thought of helping the evidence

along by freeing the bolts before you see the engineer, forget it,' I told him. Angus was always prone to gild the lily. 'But you could suddenly remember you left the keys in the dash.'

'I already told them I didn't.'

'But you weren't on oath. You were upset. They put pressure on you. They put words in your mouth.' Angus still looked doubtful. 'For God's sake,' I said, 'you never had difficulty lying to me. I remember you looking me in the eye and telling me that Duggan had tripped and fallen on his face when I knew perfectly well that he'd tried to take on Big Jim Paterson in a fight for the favours of one of the NAAFI staff. Next, I want to know who you were meeting in the bar that night. And why you wouldn't tell the police.'

'You'll keep it under your hat?'

'I won't go rushing to the police with it,' I said. 'Beyond that, I can't make any promises. I may want to talk with him.'

'I promised him on the phone I wouldn't tell about him. He doesn't want to be fashed wi' a lot of police about the place and hanging around a courtroom. And he's a man wi' a whole lot of clout around here. I want to keep in wi' him.'

'You're not telling the police, you're telling me. He may have seen the murderer.'

'I ken that,' he said. He stared at me gloomily. 'He was Mr de Forgan, the owner of Foleyknowe House and Estate. I wanted to tie up some details of the agreement, so he said he'd look in on the way back from a business appointment.'

'What sort of details?'

'Well, f'r instance, as part of the deal he wants to retain the right to hold three shoots of his own each season, maximum a hundred and fifty birds each time.'

'That's fairly normal,' I said.

'Maybe.' There was a self-satisfied glint in Angus's eye. 'I beat him down to two at a hundred and we shook hands

77

on it. He only wants to entertain his business associates and show himself off as landed gentry, he doesn't really give a damn. He's a city man who happens to live in the country. His dad left him the place, including three farms, but he leaves the running of it to his wife. Between ourselves, I reckon she's twice the countryman he is. Before he came into the place, he was already managing his uncle's jute mill, and he inherited that in the end. It's not jute now, of course. Polypropylene and the like. Diversified.'

'A pub at Hogmanay was a funny time for a business discussion,' I said.

'Och, the man has his finger in a dozen other pies, always out and about all day and half the night. You have to catch him when you can. But it's not him we should be discussing,' Angus said with a touch of his old fire, 'it's the shoot. I need to know whether you're in or not. Whatever you say, your women will go along with you.'

I could hardly say that that might depend on whether he retained his liberty. 'I may not be fit to hump bags of feed around the place,' I said.

He cast up his eyes to the ceiling. If his face was partly hidden by beard his receding hairline left the whole of his scowl on view. 'No problem,' he said impatiently. 'For when I can't get there, I've got one of those three-wheel ATVs you can use. You'll be amazed what those little buggers can carry.'

There was only one way to calm him down so that he could think rationally about his predicament. 'I'll go and take a look at the land as soon as I'm up and about,' I said. 'If it's as good as you say, we're in.'

If I had gone by the doctor's advice, Beth's wishes, and my own inclinations, I would have spent several days in bed, recovering my strength slowly and being waited on hand and foot.

But the household would be hard pressed enough to cope short-handed without the added burden of trays to be carried up and down stairs. Besides, I knew from experience that the longer I lay still the greater would be the temptation to put off a return to real life. I accepted my lunch on a tray and then struggled into trousers and a sweater over my pyjamas and, with female protests buzzing round my ears, felt my way carefully down the banisters and into the kitchen.

That was quite enough hard work for the moment. I lowered myself into one of the basket chairs.

Daffy disappeared with a basin full of puppy-meal. Beth returned some of her attention to Sam's bodily needs, but still had some to spare for my misdeeds. 'You've got to be out of your mind,' she said.

'It's warmer down here than up there,' I pointed out. 'Where's Isobel?'

'Gone to the Moss to give our two hopefuls a final orientation. Henry's gone along to shoot for her. They're setting off tomorrow.'

'Tomorrow?' Time, as usual, had slipped away faster than I could register it.

'The championships start the day after.'

In the long term, success or failure in major competitions could have a substantial effect on our profits, but there was no point getting uptight about it just yet. 'Have you tracked down any more of the cocker pups?' I asked.

Beth looked up from powdering Sam's behind. 'Of course, I've had all the time in the world for telephoning,' she said bitterly.

'Sorry,' I said.

'Don't laugh at me. Besides, I knew you'd have kittens if I did the phoning during the expensive rate, but that's finished now. While you're sitting there, you may as well try the numbers again. It won't cost anything if you don't get an answer. You've met most of the professionals at one time or another, so they won't mind talking to you.'

'What line have you been taking?' I asked her.

'If we got through to a purchaser, we mostly said that we were calling up on behalf of the breeder to remind them to keep the pup away from other dogs until it's been vaccinated. OK?'

'I think that that's within my powers,' I said.

'Would it also be within your powers to watch Sam? I must give Daffy a hand. It's pissing wet out there, but life has to go on and dogs have to be dried.'

As soon as Beth was out of the door Sam, who had been comatose during her administrations, chose to wake up and demand attention. He had already been fed and burped and he was clean and dry. I tried to explain that there was little more I could do for him, but he seemed unimpressed. So I picked him up and leaned back in the basket chair and he dozed off quite happily lying face down on my chest while I telephoned the outstanding breeders and purchasers. One breeder mentioned another and for a while it seemed that the list was becoming longer rather than shorter.

By late afternoon I had eliminated them all except for one breeder who was said to have obtained a litter of six, all black, at about the right time.

Beth returned and relieved me of Sam while I was verifying the number with Directory Enquiries. A few minutes later Isobel and Henry came in. Henry leaned his bagged gun in the corner.

Isobel had her hands behind her back. 'Which hand will you have?' she asked.

'Left,' said Beth, without looking up from her preparations for dinner.

Isobel gave a disappointed grunt and deposited a mallard drake on the table. 'You may as well have these as well, for the dogs,' she said, putting down a pair of rabbits from the other hand. 'Henry had his eye in – for once.'

'For three times,' I said.

'Should you be down here?' Isobel asked. 'The dogs were good,' she added, without awaiting an answer. 'As you said, Rowan's still over-eager and needs to blow off steam before he settles down to work. Otherwise, we're in with a chance.'

It was time for our end of the day drinks. Henry had wandered through to the sitting room. He came back with the necessary bottles, trying to look as though he had gathered them up in an absent-minded moment.

'When are you setting off?' I asked.

'First thing in the morning,' Isobel said. 'We'll come here to collect the dogs, transfer to your car and leave ours with you. Daffy's parcelling up the dogs' meals. I suppose that old rattletrap of yours will get us there?'

'There and back,' I said, 'if Rex doesn't run out of road.' My car might have seen better days but it was mechanically sound. Henry's was a newer and smarter hatchback but space would have been very cramped and the car underpowered with passengers, luggage, and dogs aboard. 'I suppose you've remembered to book a room for Rex?'

'We were going to,' Isobel said. 'God knows I didn't fancy being seen around a respectable hotel with somebody who looks as though he lives by mugging children for their sweetie-money. The Tourist Office got us the numbers of some bed and breakfast places although I wasn't confident that they'd let him in the door. But he decided of his own accord to take along his sleeping-bag and sleep in the car, which at least relieves us of any worries about the dogs.'

'He'll have to eat,' Beth pointed out.

'We can smuggle him out a doggy-bag,' Henry said.

I was only half listening. 'Which way are you going?' I asked.

Henry shrugged. 'Perth and Stirling, probably,' he said.

'You could go by Kinross and the Kincardine Bridge.'

'We could,' Henry said. 'But is there any reason why we should?'

'Yes, I think there is.' I took a drink. I prefer whisky to beer when I am low. The spirit relaxed me and brought on a yawn. 'We've covered every likely litter of cocker pups between about Inverness and Lanark. Except one. There's a lady on the outskirts of Kinross who keeps on

81

not answering her phone. It wouldn't add more than minutes to your journey to call in there and find out if she's moved away.'

'That's a good idea,' Beth said. 'But I've been thinking. People do buy dogs sometimes from a long way off. We send pups all over the place.'

'That's on the basis of reputation,' Isobel said. 'There haven't been many big names in the cocker world recently.'

Beth was hardly listening. She was watching me closely. 'You two finish your drinks and run along,' she said. 'I want to shoot some food into John and get him back to bed. If he flakes out in that chair, I'll never get him up the stairs.'

Although my long-term recovery after my illness might have left me liable to sudden setbacks, at least, as I had told Angus, the speed of my recovery from those setbacks was improving. Next morning, I dressed myself and pottered downstairs entirely under my own steam.

Beth questioned me severely and I managed to satisfy her that I was well on the mend, but she and Daffy formed the usual female alliance to forbid me from venturing outdoors. Isobel, Henry, Rowan, Lob and Rex had already left, taking with them our hopes and good wishes. Beth and Daffy seemed to be running hard to stay in one place, so they allowed me to lift some of the burden off them by taking over all the indoor duties. I spent the morning mixing puppy-food, cooking, dealing with the mail, answering the phone, and trying to keep Sam fed, clean, and amused. It was more tiring than a day spent out with the dogs, but warmer.

Daffy was always an eccentric eater, partly because she worked on the run in order to make time for Rex. When she was not joining him for a midday snack she could be seen darting around the kennels with a sandwich, a cold pork pie or a raw carrot in one hand and an opened tin of Coke dribbling into her pocket. That day, however,

Rex being far away and getting further by the minute, she agreed to join us at the lunch table. But she was still restless and when the phone rang again she jumped up to answer it before either of us could move.

The call was evidently Rex. After a few veiled but amorous allusions, she asked, 'How far have you got? . . . You're over the Border then.' She listened while still managing to munch on a filled roll. 'I'll pass it on,' she said and after a few more exchanges of sexual *badinage* she hung up and returned to her seat.

'Rex said to tell you that they stopped for petrol, coffee, and a dog-pee at Kinross Services, but when they asked their way to Mrs Bluitt's smallholding they were told that there was a fire there the night before last. Seems like she died in it. So they've gone on.'

'There wasn't anything in the papers,' Beth said.

'It would be outside the territory of the *Courier and Advertiser,*' I said, 'and not a big enough disaster for national TV. I think I'd better go through and sniff around. Somebody may know who bought her pups.'

'You're not driving anywhere until you're steadier on your pins,' Beth said. 'Especially not in Henry's car. I wouldn't mind so much if you crashed our one. The insurance money would at least give us a deposit on something that could run on unleaded.'

I was almost sure that she was joking, so I ignored the implied unconcern for my life and limb. 'You drive me, then,' I said.

Beth looked at me, at Daffy, and then at Sam. Her thoughts were so clear that they might have been stencilled on her forehead. I was still shaky and she was busy. The dogs came first and Angus and his problems a long way behind. 'You must know somebody around there who could ask your questions for you.'

I was about to deny it when I remembered that somebody had settled up recently with a cheque on a Kinross bank. I applied my own version of Pelmanism and came up with a name. 'Allan Forsyth,' I said. 'The man who brought a pup back for retraining.'

'One of Moonbeam's,' Beth said. 'Liver and white. Call him this evening.'

'Try this afternoon,' Daffy said. 'He's in the hotel trade, so that's when he might be at home. If you don't get him, try the Regis Hotel tonight. His family owns it and he's the manager.' She rarely spoke to clients but always seemed to know more about them than we did.

I found Allan Forsyth's number in our records and dialled it in mid-afternoon. His voice answered, giving only the number and sounding, for him, irritable. I had forgotten that hotel staff work late and often snatch sleep in the afternoons. 'Did I wake you?' I asked.

'Not really.' I heard him yawn. 'I was just waking up of my own accord and planning a dog-walk. Who is this?'

'John Cunningham. How are you getting on with Gorse?'

'I took him on the shoot—'

'I thought I told you—' I began.

'But I went without a gun,' he said quickly. 'I concentrated on him, just as you told me. He was perfect all morning. He tried to play me up in the afternoon so I kept him on the lead.'

'That's the right treatment,' I said. Maybe Mr Morgan was wrong and Allan Forsyth would make something of Gorse after all. 'I'm calling about a lady out your way, a Mrs Bluitt. I understand that there was a fire?'

'That's right. Poor old soul!' He was of an age at which anyone over forty is old. 'She was trapped and died in the blaze. They could see her at an upstairs window but they couldn't get her out in time. A shame. She was a nice person. A widow, one of those quiet women with a warm glow round them, know what I mean?'

'Yes, I do,' I said. Beth was surrounded by a warm glow. So was Henry. Of Isobel I was less sure.

'I knew her quite well,' Allan said. 'She did a little market-gardening and bred working cockers. I bought some of her produce and I used to meet her quite often, walking our respective dogs. We talked about dog training and she told me much the same as you did.'

'What we tell you three times is true,' I misquoted.

'I suppose it must be. Sometimes she'd come in for a bar lunch or just a shandy. Other times, she asked me to keep the pigeons off her vegetables or have a clear-out of the rabbits.' I heard him sigh. 'A terrible way to go,' he said.

I had been on the point of accepting the death at face value, but his last phrase set bells ringing. There had been other deaths to fit that description. 'How did the fire start?' I asked.

'Nobody seems to be quite sure. According to the local rag, the police say that their enquiries are continuing – whatever that means, if anything. Bar gossip has it that there was petrol involved although nobody can think of a reason why she should have petrol in the house. She kept her Rotavator in a shed about fifty yards away.'

He said 'Hullo?' twice while I picked my way through a series of unpleasant thoughts and wondered how to go on. 'You wouldn't happen to know whether she'd disposed of her last litter?' I enquired at last.

'So that's it. Getting into cockers? I was wondering why you should be interested. No, I couldn't tell you. Her sister would probably know. Hang on a moment while I get the number for you.' He rambled on absently while he looked up the number. 'A Mrs Radbone. She married a farmer whose land almost adjoins the smallholding. He ploughs – ploughed – and harrowed it for her every winter or she could never have managed to do market gardening and breed cockers, all more or less on her own. Here we are!'

He read out the phone number. I noted it down and thanked him. 'I'll get in touch with her,' I said. 'If you hear any more bar gossip about the fire, give me a ring.'

'I'll do that,' he said. We chatted about dogs for a few seconds and rang off.

SIX

I tried the number of the Radbones' farm but only made contact with an answering machine with a strong Scots accent. I left a message, giving my name and phone number but saying that I would phone again.

It was time for the main meal, entailing a whole variety of diets for the different groups of puppies, young dogs, nursing dams, and two pregnant bitches, one of them almost due to whelp. Daffy came in, loaded the steaming bowls onto a trolley, and departed.

'*How would you like to be,*' she was singing as she worked, '*Slightly insane with me. Oh what I'd give for an hou-er or two, Going completely bananas with you.*'

It took me several days to get that version of the old song out of my head.

I opened a window to let the various dogfood smells clear and took a dish through to the pup in the surgery. He greeted me as a long-lost friend and attacked the dish as though starving.

We had never given him a name. He was already responding to 'Pup' and seemed to be more intelligent than many springers of the same age. Dealing with dogs day in and day out, one can become blasé and begin to think of them as no more than a commodity, but sooner or later a dog will turn up that jerks one back to the knowledge that they have charm and character – and needs. Pup was such a one. He was a cheerful little dog, growing visibly. He should have been moved out to one of the isolation kennels by now except that we would need space for the returning competitors and any dogs left for training. There were too many pups around, still too young for their full complement of shots, for us to risk the importation of kennel-cough or Parvo virus or worse. I spent a few minutes playing with him, improvising a game with an old sock.

I was wondering whether we shouldn't diversify into cockers of working strains. They are quick and cheerful dogs with excellent noses, though sometimes headstrong, and their small size, although a handicap when it comes to retrieving a hare or a goose, lets them penetrate deeper into tight cover than larger dogs.

My reverie and our game were interrupted by the phone. Isobel was calling to report their safe arrival at the nearest hotel to the championship venue. I reiterated our wishes for good luck. In field trials, good luck is almost as necessary as good training and handling.

Following the instructions that Beth had given me I began to prepare our evening meal; but she came in soon afterwards, shedding wet oilskins and the smell of the great outdoors. She checked on Sam, decided that all was well, and sent me back to my basket. Basket chair, I mean.

The phone kept me occupied. I fobbed off two enquirers after pups but was careful to get their numbers. In fact, we had a litter of which the two that we had decided not to train on would soon be old enough to go, but they had been sired by Rowan and a good performance in the championships would justify a premium on the price. Another enquirer, an elderly man who had more sense and compassion than to start afresh with a young dog when his own remaining active years might be few, was ready to make an offer for a retired brood bitch and former field-trial winner. We closed the deal over the phone.

The phone rang again. I picked it up, expecting another enquirer. 'Throaks Kennels,' I said.

'This is Mrs Radbone,' said a broad, female voice.

The name meant nothing to me for a moment, but the accent provided a hint. Mrs Bluitt's sister. 'Thank you for calling me back,' I said. 'I was very sorry to hear about your sister.'

'Aye. It was sad,' she said and waited patiently for me to go on.

I was still wondering what to say when I heard myself saying it. 'I was interested to know what homes her last litter of pups went to,' I said. 'I suppose all her paperwork was destroyed in the fire?'

'Aye. It was that.'

'She never mentioned any of the names to you?'

'Not that I mind. The pups are all away. I'm just left with her three bitches. They were in an outside run and the fire didn't touch them.' I heard her sigh. 'But what to do with them I don't know. My man keeps collies, and rough beasts they are, some of them. They don't get along with the cockers at all.'

'We could board them for you while you think about it,' I suggested. If she took me up on it, our own two would have to go into one of the whelping kennels.

'Och,' she said, 'I'm not wanting to run up a lot of expense when I've no mind to keep them. If you've a kennels, would you not care to make me an offer for them?'

I was struck dumb by the suddenness of the suggestion. After a few seconds of silence, she went on. 'Come away now. A hundred pounds for the three of them. What do you say?'

The late Mrs Bluitt had neither worked nor competed with her own stock, but I knew her kennel name and the strains were good. I had seen dogs of her breeding figure in the frame at 'Any Variety of Spaniel' trials. At a hundred pounds, it could be the thief's bargain of the decade.

'How often have they been bred from?' I asked.

'Not one of them's had more than two litters.'

The Kennel Club would be able to furnish the missing

pedigrees. 'Done,' I said. 'I'll post you a cheque straight away.'

'And come for them? I want them off my hands. I can't take them home or there'll be blood shed and I'm scunnered of traipsing to and fro with food for them.'

'Somebody will be in-by in the next few days,' I said.

'There's just one thing. One of them's pregnant. Do you mind?'

'Not in the least,' I said. A pregnant cocker bitch of good working stock would be as good as money in the bank. A few enquiries would soon identify the sire. 'But I'm still interested in the whereabouts of the last litter. You can't call to mind anything your sister said?'

'She never spoke much about them. The one thing I do mind is that they were all spoken for before Christmas and deposits paid. They'd be for presents, likely. But one purchaser cried off. And then another brought back the pup the next day. My sister aye made it clear that she'd take them back at half price if the family changed their minds, rather than have the pup passed on to a bad home or just abandoned.'

'I do the same,' I said with feeling.

'Aye. Well, there she was with two pups on her hands, but before she could get around to advertising them a mannie phoned wanting one and fetched it the same day. Then, two days later, at Hogmanay it was, wasn't he on the phone again saying he'd take the other one and he was coming through straight away?'

'But she didn't mention his name?' I found that my voice came out in a gasp and realized that I had been holding my breath.

'I haven't finished,' she said. 'But no, she never said who he was. But she said that he was on the phone again the very next day, asking didn't she know where to put her hands on a third. It was just you calling up about the same pups that brought it back to me.'

I thanked her sincerely, repeated my promises, and disconnected.

Beth had come in. 'What have you let us in for now?' she asked.

'It's a safe bet that both those pups came from Kinross,' I told her.

'Oh. What have you—?'

'And the same man tried to buy a third one.'

'Very interesting. What were you spending our money on?'

She was not going to give up. 'I've bought the late Mrs Bluitt's three brood bitches,' I said.

Beth hit the ceiling.

The next morning was a definite drag. I was feeling almost back to normal but the female coalition limited me to an hour or so on the lawn – and that only because the day was dry and they needed my help. Several of the younger dogs in training were at a stage requiring regular exposure to flushing game. For lack of access to suitable ground, I had created a variety of complicated devices, designed to simulate flushing birds or bolting rabbits. These, however, were too idiosyncratic in design for Beth to set up, but when my pheasant-skin dummy had rocketed satisfactorily a dozen times, with satisfactory responses from the pupils, I was dismissed back to the house. I would have been roused into rebellion except that I was still manoeuvring towards acceptance of the cocker spaniels

For once, Daffy was almost my ally. She accepted the imminent arrival of three more brood bitches calmly and planned a sensible reallocation of the whelping and isolation kennels. Beth was irritable and working it off on me. I had no right to commit the partnership to capital outlay, running expenditure, and hard work without consultation. She was right, but that did not make it any easier to accept her strictures without snapping back.

Mrs Radbone phoned again at lunchtime. By some miraculous working of the Post Office my cheque had arrived; but when was I coming to fetch those dratted

90

dogs of her sister's? I said that I'd come over that afternoon.

'You are not fit to drive,' Beth said. 'And I have the keys of Henry's car.'

'Come and drive me,' I said.

'I can't spare the time. Henry and Isobel will be coming back that way.'

'Not for a couple of days. Mrs Radbone's getting impatient.' I decided that two could be as crabby as one and that I might as well get my turn over while Beth was still in the dumps. That way, we could recover together. 'I'll take a taxi,' I added.

Daffy, who was again sharing lunch with us, stepped in quickly. 'I can manage for the afternoon. You go, Mrs Cunningham. The break will do you good.'

'You're sure?'

'How long will it take you?' Daffy asked rhetorically. 'Forty minutes each way? Two hours altogether, three at the most. Why wouldn't I cope?' She contrived to sound insulted but she winked at me behind Beth's back.

I called Mrs Radbone back to say that we were coming. We strapped Sam's Carricot onto the back seat of Henry's hatchback and put a large dogbed in the boot, leaving the parcel shelf in the house. The car stood on its nose once or twice until Beth adjusted to the automatic transmission and stopped declutching with the brake pedal.

The drive to Kinrose took longer than Daffy's forty minutes because of road-works. 'I wonder how Isobel's getting on,' I said, as we sat and glared at a red traffic light which only glared back at us while nothing whatever came the other way.

'As Isobel says, knowing wouldn't change anything. She'll phone tonight,' Beth said grimly. 'Just you wait till she hears that we've branched out into cockers.'

'If she grizzles about it the way you're doing,' I said, 'I'll pay the hundred quid out of my own pocket and keep them as my personal dogs.'

'You wouldn't!'

91

'Why not? You do,' I pointed out. Beth had a Labrador of her own and was still striving to make him up to champion.

She was silent as far as the next traffic control. I had flicked her on the raw. We had given her every encouragement, but she felt guilty about the time she devoted to Jason. 'I don't really grizzle, do I?' she asked in a small voice.

'Only a little bit,' I said. 'A mini-grizzle now and again. And again.'

We were nearing Kinross before she spoke again. 'I wonder how Isobel's getting on,' she said. It was a peace offering.

The burned-out shell of Mrs Bluitt's house was like a wound against the blue sky. The sheds and pens at the side of what had been a neat garden, before the fire brigade flattened it, had escaped the flames. Mrs Radbone was waiting. She introduced us to the three cocker bitches, beautiful little dogs with silky coats and liquid eyes. Their settled world had been turned upside-down. They were nervous and in desperate need of reassurance but we coaxed them into the boot of the hatchback, soothed them with titbits and kind words and waited until they were settled. Beth tried to look disapproving but I could see that she was already smitten.

'I'm glad to see the back of them,' Mrs Radbone said, 'and yet I'm sorry to see them go. It's as if it's the end of Stella.' She fumbled in the waistband of her skirt for a handkerchief. 'I suppose I shouldn't really displenish them until her will's proved, but she left me everything. And it breaks my heart to keep coming here.' She glanced once at the ruined house and looked away. 'Go now, quickly.'

We got back on the motorway. 'Go round by Perth,' I said. 'It's not much further and it's dual carriageway until we're almost home. We can miss those road-works.'

'All right.' She was silent for a couple of miles. 'If the police decided that she had something to do with her sister's death,' she said suddenly, 'the sale could be invalidated.'

'It won't happen,' I told her. 'The smallholding without the house can't be worth very much and somebody else had a stronger motive for wanting Mrs Bluitt silenced. If I can see that, so can the police.'

'They'll probably blame Angus,' she said, which started me thinking again.

Henry's hatchback cruised along at an easy seventy. I waited until we were past Perth and heading for Dundee. 'Foleyknowe's only a few miles out of our road,' I said. 'Let's take a look at the shoot.'

I saw Beth glance at the dashboard clock and then look in the mirror at Sam, who was deeply asleep. 'You intended this all along, didn't you?' she said.

'It'll save us making another trip.'

'You did, then.'

But she turned off where I told her to. After a few miles we took to a driveway, bypassed a substantial house which had the blank look of the temporarily empty and followed a rough estate-road to park where a stand of tall conifers had been planted to give the house shelter from the prevailing wind. The dogs in the back of the car sat up, wondering where we had arrived.

The conifers were the only mature trees to be seen, but we were at the junction of two diverging valleys along which, as Angus had said, the cover was fenced against cattle. Among the bushes, treeguards drew my eye to a host of saplings, now bare but reaching their thin branches skyward. In my mind's eye I could see the strips of game crops on the higher ground and the feeders that would lead the birds up to them.

The low sun was still finding its way under the branches or I might not have noticed a shed almost lost among the trees and screened by ivy. I got out of the car and walked over to it. The door was locked but the post was rotten and a good push opened it. All that I could see in the semi-darkness was that the shed was empty except for a stack of old straw bales at one end, but it seemed dry and sound enough to house the equipment that a shoot would need. I pulled the door closed, making a mental note to apologize for the damage at a more suitable moment, and came back to the car.

'All right,' I said. 'Let's go home.'

'Don't you want to look around?'

I was feeling tired. 'I've looked,' I said. 'In a year or two, this bit will be perfect. I'll take Angus's word for it that the rest is much the same.'

With much toing and froing, Beth turned the car in a field gate. The rear of the house was facing us and in my peripheral vision I saw a movement, perhaps a curtain being drawn. So the house was not empty.

Beth must have noticed the same movement. 'Shouldn't we call at the house?'

'Isobel will be phoning soon.'

A progress report was more important than a courtesy call. Beth set off for home.

'You think we should take it on, then?' she asked as we turned out of the driveway.

'It depends,' I said.

Beth slowed in the narrow road to let a Jaguar, driven by a woman and with two children in the back, squeeze past. 'Depends on what?' she asked.

My attention had been drawn to a springer pup on the knee of the girl child in the other car and I had to bring it back. 'Firstly on whether Angus stays out of gaol.'

'And if he does, what else?'

'Satisfactory agreement with the farmers about planting game crops. And some shed space. That's all I can think of for the moment.'

Sam woke up and announced in no uncertain terms that he was starving to death. Beth made all speed for Dundee, the Tay Road Bridge, and home.

The sun was down but Daffy was only slightly anxious by the time we arrived. Nobody had phoned.

I was detailed to attend to Sam and to begin preparations for our meal while Beth and Daffy checked over the newcomers, included them in the distribution of food, and installed them together in a spare whelping kennel. They might be cramped but they would draw comfort from each other amid a host of larger and boistrous springers.

Sam accepted my efforts tolerantly but showed surprise. 'Get used to it, buddy,' I told him. 'You're not the Latest Arrival any more.'

Beth came in eventually and took over. As usual, she talked steadily while she flitted between Sam and the stove. 'They're adorable,' she said. 'But cockers don't fetch the same price as springers.'

'They do,' I said. 'And they eat less. But it's a more selective market. We can always sell them off if we don't want to diversify. We could show a profit on them any day of the week.'

Beth looked at the clock. 'The championship must have finished for the day ages ago,' she said. 'Why hasn't somebody phoned? Are you going to tell the police what Mrs Whoosit said about the man who bought two pups and wanted another?'

I had been wondering the same thing. Her question helped me to make up my mind. 'I'll have to. It may not help Angus much. We'll just have to hope that he has an alibi this time.'

'You could ask him first,' Beth suggested.

'We'll have to tell them anyway. If Angus is innocent, the truth is his best defence.'

I had no idea how to get hold of DCI Kipple, so I phoned Constable Peel and told him to pass the word on. 'We have Mrs Bluitt's bitches here,' I added. 'If it becomes relevant, it wouldn't be difficult to prove whether one of them was the dam of that pup.'

'Are you going to do that?' he asked.

'If it suits your cousin's defence. Otherwise, let the police spend their money.'

The phone rang a few minutes later while Beth was out

of the room answering a cry from Sam. Isobel was on the line. She sounded slightly pickled, which explained the delay in phoning. I switched on the amplifier so that Beth would be able to hear.

'Both dogs are going forward to the second day,' Isobel said. 'I thought for a minute that Rowan had blown it and was going to be eliminated. He was hunting a pile of brashings where another dog had already put out a hen pheasant. I could see that the judge was getting impatient. He thought that Rowan was being fooled by the scent left by the hen. So did I, to be honest. But I remembered you saying to trust the dog. He put out another pheasant, a cock. The nearer gun only winged it, a strong runner in thick cover. Rowan seemed to me to be taking the heel-scent. I tried to turn him and he ignored me for a moment. Then, when he turned back, the judge said that I was wrong and the dog had been right first time.'

'That sounds like Dan Pringle,' I said. Pringle was inclined to give unwanted advice to the handlers, often wrongly.

'That's who it was. I wasn't going to change my mind or I'd have been on a hiding to nothing, but I was sweating big drops. Then Rowan popped out of some rhododendrons with the bird in his jaws. I've never been more relieved in my life. I could have burst into song.'

'But you didn't, I hope.'

'No. For two gins I would have done. But the gins were still in the future at that time. How are things, back at the ranch?'

I told her about my purchase of the late Mrs Bluitt's bitches.

Isobel repeated the kennel name thoughtfully. Drunk or sober, her knowledge and recall of gun-dog breeding lines is unequalled. 'That's good stock,' she said. 'How much did you give for them?'

'A hundred.'

'What?' Isobel's voice was a squawk. For a moment, I thought that she was objecting to the disbursement of such a large sum. 'For the three? One of them in pup? I suppose you made the poor woman throw in her virtue and a diamond necklace as a makeweight?'

'You agree, then?'

'At the price, I'd probably have handed over the cheque so quickly I'd have broken her arm. Are we going to train cockers on now, and compete with them?'

'That's for discussion,' I told her. 'If you don't want to spread yourself, Beth might like to take it on.'

'We'll see,' Isobel said. 'Give her my love.'

'Go easy on the bottle,' I said. 'You'll need a clear head in the morning.' I heard her hang up. The click sounded indignant.

Beth had returned. 'Well?' she said. 'I missed some of that.'

'She thinks I got a bargain. And she sends her love.'

'That isn't what I meant and you know it.'

I relented. 'Both dogs go forward to tomorrow.'

'Whee!' Beth sat down very lightly on my knee and kissed my nose. 'Unless they make a pig's breakfast tomorrow, that should mean Certificates of Merit at least. What were you saying I might take on?'

'Handling cockers in competition.'

She jumped off my knee as though it had become red hot and stirred something furiously at the stove. 'I have Sam now,' she said.

'I'd expect Sam to be toddling before the first pups are mature enough for field trials,' I pointed out.

She stirred some more, splashing something greasy onto the tiles behind the stove. 'I'd be scared of letting you down,' she said at last.

'But you already compete with Jason in retriever stakes,' I said.

'But that's for me. If I blow it, it doesn't affect the business.'

'You never do blow it. You stay as calm as Isobel. And the spaniels work well for you in training. You're good.'

She turned pink and regarded me with a mixture of suspicion and hope. 'Am I really?'

'All right,' I said. 'Don't believe me. Ask Isobel. I

97

haven't had a good look at the new ones yet. I think I'll take a walk and see how they're settling in.'

Beth switched instantly from hesitation to her bossy mode. 'They're settling in fine and you're not going out in the night air yet. You can walk them in the morning, if it's fine. We won't want them to meet the other dogs yet. Do you think the puppy would be more at home if we moved him in with them? He'd still recognize his dam.'

'If she is his dam,' I said. 'We can't be sure yet. Leave it a little longer.'

I got down to phoning the vets around Kinross to find out whether the immunizations of our new acquisitions were up to date.

Beth wanted to pack me off to bed for another early night, but I was feeling fully recovered and sleep was a long way off. Besides, there was a play on television that I wanted to see. I settled, reclining on the settee in the sitting room, with a fire of beech logs sending ripples of light around the room. Outside, the wind was rising, drawing sparks up the chimney. Beth joined me on the settee and took my legs across her lap. We were back in harmony.

It was too good to last. The play was just becoming convoluted enough to grip me when the phone rang and the evening began to go mad.

The first caller was a distraught Mrs Radbone. A local sergeant of police had called and, while milking her of every word she could remember her sister saying about the purchases of pups, had contrived, first, to let slip that her sister's death was now being treated as a case of murder and then to let her think that I had accused her of something dread but unspecified. My attempts at an explanation were shouted down. She wanted her sister's dogs back, but she was not going to get them from me without a struggle and I told her so. She had already paid my cheque into her bank and, although she had anticipated probate and the sale was therefore of questionable legality, if the law moved at its customary pace the death would be solved and the dogs probably retired before she could do anything about it.

She hung up on me at last and I was just picking up the threads of the television play when Angus phoned. He had been at home, overhauling his incubators and brooders to be ready for the busiest part of his year, when DCI Kipple had arrived with a constable in tow, showing a renewed interest in his comings and goings and hinting that I was at the bottom of it.

Angus was both suspicious and resentful until I managed to get across that I had tracked the probable source of both cocker pups and that it seemed probable that the breeder had been another on the growing list of murder victims. When it dawned on him that he had been entertaining neighbours at the time of the fire and that DCI Kipple had set out deliberately to alienate him from his only active helper, he cooled down rapidly.

'I knew you'd not let me down,' he said. 'I'm off the hook, surely.'

'It's a start,' I said. 'A procurator fiscal could argue his way around it. An accomplice of yours might have set the fire.'

'Like who?'

I nearly said 'Like me,' but decided that that was a thought I would rather keep to myself. 'I had a look at Foleyknowe on my way back from Kinross,' I said.

The change of subject brought an immediate change of mood. Even over the phone I could hear his smile. 'What did you think?'

'I think you could be right. We'd have to work in with the agents who bring parties up for a week's shooting break. At the moment they can put together a day's wildfowling, a day walking up, one day driven, and then they're scratching around and having to Range Rover them up to Perth or Deeside. But the market for second-rate shooting is swamped. We'd have to show first-class birds, so we'd be dependent on getting game crops sown on the high ground. Is that in the contract?'

'Not in writing. I thought we'd deal with the individual farmers.'

'I'd rather have it in the contract with the landowner. He can work it through the tenancy agreements and then we'd be covered. And I'd like to be sure that we had shed space and the use of a room where the visitors could lunch in bad weather. There's a brick shed tucked away among the trees which doesn't seem to be doing anything.'

'There is? I never noticed it.'

'It's there all the same.'

'Speak to him yourself, then. But do it soon, before he decides to advertise.'

We went back to the play but I had hardly sorted out the characters again in my mind when a car arrived at the door. I prepared to answer the bell but Beth jumped to her feet as soon as I lifted my knees off her. I reached for the remote control. My chances of catching up with the plot had waned to vanishing point.

She came back with Detective Chief Inspector Kipple and his attendant constable, both in 'plain clothes' – which I would have called 'mufti'.

The DCI started off in suspicious mood. He would have been prepared to conduct the interview standing but I insisted that we all sit down. He lowered his backside into one of the wingchairs as though into a cauldron.

He began by thanking us coldly for the information relayed by Constable Peel. The words must have stuck in his throat, because he followed up by enquiring just how we had traced Mrs Bluitt and her sister.

'By phoning around everyone who breeds cockers,' I said. 'There weren't so many black pups born around the right time. When we'd eliminated nearly all of them, we were left with Mrs Bluitt.'

'It didn't occur to you to let the police do their job?'

I nearly said that the police didn't seem to be doing their job worth a damn, but I bit it back. 'We were asked by Angus Todd to make enquiries—'

'Over the gun-dog grapevine,' Beth put in anxiously.

'Which might help to prove his innocence. Your enquiries seemed to be directed towards making a case against him.'

'Our enquiries are directed only towards discovering the truth,' the DCI snorted.

'So were mine,' I said. 'And I told you what I found out without waiting to see whether or not it helped to bear out Mr Todd's story.'

He did not miss the implied criticism. 'If it comes to a case,' he said, 'we're required to furnish the defence with all the evidence, whether it supports our case or not.'

'But you're not required to look for evidence that contradicts your theory,' I pointed out. 'Somebody else has to do that.' I decided to push my luck. 'In confidence, is there still any likelihood that the fire was accidental?'

He puffed out a breath of exasperation. 'If it will buy me a little co-operation, I'll tell you this – in confidence. The local Firemaster's prepared to bet his pension that petrol was squirted through the letterbox and followed by a match. Now, tell me this. On canine evidence alone, how sure can you be that the puppy in your care came from one of Mrs Bluitt's bitches?'

I was forced to hesitate. I had been assuming the relationship because of the general circumstances. But it seemed that my information was out of date.

'Fairly sure,' Beth said. 'I took the pup out to the whelping kennel.'

'You didn't tell me that,' I said.

'You were watching the play. And you'd only have gone on at me about the risk of spreading infection. Anyway, Chief Inspector, when I put the pup down he ran straight to the one that had had a recent litter. She was sick immediately. So then I knew.'

The Chief Inspector was looking dazed. 'Knew what?'

'That he was her pup.'

DCI Kipple emitted a sound of mingled enquiry and bafflement that is not capable of phonetic spelling. 'I would have thought,' he said, 'that it proved the contrary.'

'You don't understand,' Beth said gently. (The Chief Inspector shook his head.) 'After the milk's dried up, some dams, as soon as they see one of their own pups, will regurgitate food as an alternative to providing milk for them.'

'Ah!' DCI Kipple, an expression of mild revulsion on his round face, thought about it. 'If it should become important to prove the relationship, we can hardly do it by having a cocker spaniel bitch throw up all over the courtroom.'

'She'd have stopped doing it long before then anyway,' I said. 'You'd have to resort to genetic fingerprinting.'

'And were you thinking . . . ?'

'We'll leave that to you,' I said. 'As far as I know, there's only one laboratory in the country doing it privately and it costs a packet. Your forensic scientists can get it done, if and when you need it.'

'And in the mean time,' said Kipple gloomily, 'one or both of them dies of distemper or some such ailment. I'll make arrangements.'

'You are not taking the dogs away,' Beth said. 'Send somebody here and Isobel can take tissue samples in their presence.'

When the police had taken themselves off, I phoned Foleyknowe. A voice identified itself as belonging to Mr de Forgan and agreed to see me at four the following afternoon. 'Take a look around before the light goes,' he said. 'That way, we'll both know what we're talking about.'

'I'll do that,' I said. I nearly mentioned my previous visit and the damage to the shed but decided that the moment was not yet ripe. 'Did Angus tell you that he'd asked me to look into the events of Hogmanay?'

'The death of that petty crook? Yes, he mentioned it. I don't think that anything I can say will be of any help to you and I'd prefer not to waste time with the police if it can be avoided. We can discuss it when I see you.'

He sounded like a reasonable man.

SEVEN

Dogs sense when they are getting less than full attention and they soon start to play up. In the morning, my mind was on the questions which still had to be asked and where I should be asking them, and I soon saw that my training sessions were doing as much harm as good. In mid-morning I gave up, kennelled the current pupil, and went back to the house. Beth gave me a message from Angus to the effect that he had a noncommittal report on his Land-Rover from the main agent.

'I'll go over and see him,' I said. Perhaps a drive and a talk with Angus might clear my thinking.

'You could phone him.'

'I'd rather see him face to face and maybe look at the Land-Rover again.' I collected the keys and went out to Henry's car, which was sitting on the gravel in front of the house and facing the gates as if impatient to be taken for a walk.

Beth came out with me.

As I strapped myself in, I was still sifting and rearranging the few facts that we had. If my mind had been on the car, events would have been different . . . and I would almost certainly have died.

'Drive carefully,' Beth said.

'Don't I always?' I asked absently.

I turned the key in the ignition and the world went mad around me, familiarity turned on its head.

The engine fired and picked up and the car surged forward toward the gateway and the public roads.

I switched off the ignition, to no effect. I stamped on the brake pedal and jerked up the handbrake, but there was no 'feel' to either of them. I had to snatch a quick look down at the unfamiliar controls. The gear selector was at P, but when I jerked it back towards R the handle came away in my hand. I dropped it on the floor. The automatic gearbox changed up.

My thinking had been slow and it was too late to bale out into the bushes. The gateway with its stone gateposts was rushing at me. I could have slowed or halted progress while speed was still comparatively low by swerving into the shrubbery, but my mind was still disoriented and it was against my instincts to wreck Henry's car. At least the steering still seemed to work. I shot out onto the road under the nose of another car. Our gate was on a bend. The village was away to the right but ahead the road ran on through open country.

The engine was cold but, against that, the automatic choke was functioning and the car was helped by a slight downhill. The transmission shifted into top. The roadside was becoming a blur but the car held straight.

The fear of death concentrates the mind wonderfully, as Samuel Johnson pointed out. Despite the mad circumstances and our headlong rush, I was coming out of my first reaction of stunned disbelief and a part of my brain, which at first had seemed eggbound, was thinking with icy calm. Too late now to bale out. To my right was the Moss where boggy ground would have slowed us gently, but the fence was solidly posted and would probably throw us back onto the road. On my left, a stone wall fronted by solid-looking trees.

Ahead, I knew, the road rose again to a crest with a right-hand bend which I thought, given a little luck and a clear road, I could get round without too much damage. After another half-mile there was a sharp left-hander between stone walls. End of the road, for me.

But just over the crest, on the slight bend as I remembered it, there was a break in the dry-stone wall and a

104

wooden gate to a field that rose ever more steeply to a crown of gorse bushes. If I could smash through the gate I could put the car at the hill. At least it would slow us to the point where I might be able to roll out onto the grass without more than minor injuries.

The crest was in sight. Beyond it, something was beginning to grow out of the road. A tractor and trailer. In the field beyond? No, by God! It was in the middle of the road, but even if it had pulled towards the side there would never have been room for the two of us to pass. Somebody was going to have to give way, and it was unlikely to be the tractorman.

My one chance was to reach the gateway first. As near as I could judge, the tractor was almost there. If the driver saw me coming and stopped . . .

We swept up to the crest and I had an instant glimpse, instantly absorbed. There was no time for thought. The tractor had stopped just beyond the opening and the driver was down and opening the gate. The gateway was slightly to the further side of the bend so that, although I did not have a straight run at it, my swerve was less than it might have been. I jerked the wheel. The tractorman jumped for his life. The engine noise beat back at me for an instant from the stonework. The car wanted to roll over but a hump in the ground threw us back. And then I was on blessed, open grass and heading up the steepening hillside.

The car bounced, slowing as the hillside weighed us back. Part of the field had been dunged ready for spring ploughing, and a rear wheel spun for a moment, bleeding away more speed. The car changed gear once and again and doggedly climbed. The hill became steeper. Ahead was a bank, topped by bushes and peppered with holes, and I saw a wave of rabbits bolting for home. I steered straight for the bank, undoing my seat-belt and unlatching my door. If the engine stalled, anything could happen.

The car came to a halt, quite gently, against the bank, at an upward angle so steep that I could feel it settling back on its springs. The engine laboured but held it from rolling back. I struggled to push the door open against the pull of gravity and managed to roll out. The tractor was following me up the hill and I could see a car below, but I was more concerned to fix the car before its engine died. I found a few loose stones and packed them behind the wheels.

The other car had overhauled the tractor but had failed to make it up the steepest part of the slope. The driver was out and running and I saw that he was Constable Peel, in uniform. He dead-heated with the tractor.

The two men, in their differing ways, were both asking me what the hell I was playing at, but the time for discussion was not yet ripe. I wish that I could remember what I said, because it stopped them dead.

'Bring the tractor up behind the car,' I shouted. The tractorman caught on and hauled his load of dung closer until the bonnet of the tractor was just behind the car's boot. I nodded. Now if the car jumped my stones there would be some damage but not a catastrophe.

Peel, meanwhile, had leaned into the car and turned the ignition key, without perceptible result. He shot one enquiring glance at me before turning back and groping for the bonnet catch.

The tractorman wanted to bawl me out for scaring him, but I was in no mood to listen to him. Peel had the bonnet up. He jerked off the high-tension lead and the engine's racket died at last, its place taken by the hissing of steam from the overheated radiator. The car settled back but my stones held it.

Peel must have had an aptitude for things mechanical, because I had only begun to identify the main elements in the unfamiliar layout under the bonnet when he grabbed me by the elbow.

'You'd better take a look for yourself,' he said. 'Somebody doesn't like you very much.'

For the first time, I began to think about causes rather than effects. In what, for the placid Constable, passed for a frenzy of excitement, his finger was jumping around like a spaniel greeting a long-absent master, but when I managed to focus on one area at a time I saw that the throttle had been disconnected at the carburettor and the lever tied open with a scrap of string, an insulated wire had been added connecting the live terminal of the battery direct to the coil, and another wire led forward. My eyes followed where Peel was pointing. The second wire had been stripped of insulation where it had been led across the front of the car between the radiator and the grille. Two plastic bottles of some clear liquid had been wedged at either side of the same space.

Working gently, Peel detached the two wires from the battery. 'That should be a mite less lethal now,' he said.

The tractorman's indignation had turned to technical interest. He was a youngish man who, I knew, pottered with old cars at the weekends. He touched the neck of one of the bottles and sniffed his fingers. 'Petrol,' he said. 'By Christ! You weren't meant to win through.'

'That's for sure,' Peel said. 'If you'd hit anything, anything at all, and if the impact hadn't killed you, the bottles would have been crushed, there'd have been a spark, and the fire would have finished you off.'

'Nothing there that'd've taken more'n a minute or two to fix,' said the tractorman, 'and not a lot to be seen after the fire.' His foremost reaction now seemed to be admiration for the ingenuity of the trap. He lay down to look beneath the car. 'A bolt cutter could have done this to the brakes in a wink. I wonder how he jiggered your gear selector.' He seemed ready to dismantle the car on the spot to find out, but Peel checked him.

'Don't touch anything, either of you,' he said. 'Just wait.' He descended the hill to his car and I saw him speaking over the radio.

'God!' said the tractorman. He moved away from the car before lighting a crumpled cigarette. 'I thought you was going to kill the both of us. But we're both here and hale. That's cowped somebody's hurly. If I was you, I'd caa canny.'

I quite realized that somebody's plans had been spoiled

and I assured him that I had every intention of being careful. I found that my voice was a croak and now that the emergency was over my knees were shaking.

'Clever, though,' said the tractorman. 'If I'd no been there and with the yett open . . .'

I nodded. I had been trying not to picture being swept up the hill in a blazing car.

Peel came puffing back up the steep gradient. 'You,' he said to the tractorman, 'stand guard for a few minutes while I give Mr Cunningham a run home. If anybody comes, don't let them near the car and tell them nothing.'

'I can wait until reinforcements arrive,' I said.

He looked at me reprovingly. 'Your wife will be frantic,' he said.

I had forgotten that Beth had seen my headlong departure. I hurried to the police Escort with him. He backed the car down the worst of the gradient before trying to turn. I could feel the car trying to roll over. Peel concentrated in a grim silence until he had the car heading safely down the hill in bottom gear.

'That's Mr Kitts's car, isn't it?'

'He and Isobel are away in mine,' I said.

'Where does he usually get his work done?'

'At the service station.'

'When we've finished examining it, I'll call them and have them collect it.' Peel nursed the car onto the road and set off slowly back in the direction of Three Oaks. 'Who was the trap meant for?'

I had been wondering the same thing. 'Me, I suppose. But the first driver could as easily have been Beth.'

'Can you think of any motive for killing either of you, except that you've been asking the right questions?'

'Damned if I can,' I said.

'So what questions have you been asking that might have spelled danger for somebody?'

'Only about dogs and puppies, that I can think of.'

A small figure appeared ahead, running towards us along the verge. 'Better tell your wife as little as possible,' Peel said.

'She won't let me rest until she knows it all,' I told him. 'And she wouldn't be fooled by a pack of lies.'

He pulled up just short of her and I got out. Beth threw herself into my arms. I could feel her heart pounding and she was gasping for breath. 'What . . . what happened? What were you doing?'

'I'll tell you in the car,' I said.

'You're all right?'

'Perfectly.'

'And Henry's car?'

'More or less the same, except that somebody buggered about with it. I didn't drive off like that on purpose.' I put her into the back of the police Escort and sat in beside her.

'Somebody tried to kill you,' Beth said in a small voice. 'Is that what you're saying?'

'Not necessarily,' Peel said over his shoulder. 'Somebody rigged an accident that could have killed or injured either of you. Or either Mr or Mrs Kitts if you didn't use the car again before they returned.'

'You make him sound like a maniac shooting into a crowd,' I said.

'He may have meant to frighten you off, or to keep you too busy and upset to mess in his business. You've been lucky. You haven't been harmed, but the warning reached you.' His voice changed gear. 'Maybe Angus is asking too much of you.'

I thought it over while Peel nosed up our drive and turned the car at the door. Daffy, with Sam strapped on her back and evidently asleep, was supervising a host of pups on the clean grass. When she saw that all was well, she gave us a wave and returned her attention to the pups.

'No,' I said at last. 'If Angus needs my help, he'll have it. Nobody's going to talk freely to him while it's known that he's under suspicion, so he needs somebody nosing around who isn't just trying to prove him guilty. Not that I seem to be doing a damn bit of good.'

'If somebody thinks you are,' Beth said, 'that might be a starting point. If you're sure you have to go on.'

109

'I'm sure.'

'I don't want you to get yourself killed.'

'I don't want to be killed,' I assured her with feeling. 'But if somebody already thinks that I'm a danger to him, the quickest way to get safe is to help bring the whole thing to the right end. I just can't think what the hell I've done that could worry anybody the least bit. I'm at a dead end.'

'That's what I meant,' Beth said. 'What's happened tells you that something you've said or done or found out is very dangerous to somebody. All you've got to do is to work out what it is.'

'You'll be careful?' Peel asked seriously. He turned round in his seat to watch our faces.

'That's what I was going to say,' said Beth.

'Believe me,' I said, 'I'm going to watch my back and stay out of the shadows.'

'In that case,' Peel said, 'I'll tell you what I was coming here to tell you when you came scooting past me. And, remember, you didn't get it from me. My cousin isn't the only man the police are taking a hard look at. The dead woman's husband, Mr Wentworth, has a Land-Rover. He's in agricultural chemicals. His Land-Rover's been examined. It's taken a lot of knocks in its time but it's remarkably clean.'

'Oh?' I said, 'or something equally penetrating.

'Just listen. He claims to have been up north when his wife was killed. If that's true, it's hard to credit him with any motive for the killing at Hogmanay. DCIs Straun and Kipple have been using the police office here as a meeting ground between Dundee and Kirkcaldy, and Wentworth has to visit a farmer over here this afternoon, so they've arranged to see him here and go over his statement for the nth time. He's probably in my office now. It's a fair bet that he'll take a bar lunch at the hotel. If you happened to be taking a snack there yourself, you couldn't miss him. A tall man, fair haired, and looks as though he got out of the wrong side of somebody else's bed this and

110

every other morning. At the very least, you could see if he jogs your memory. He may have shown his face in the bar that night.

'And now, I see a blue light flashing beyond the village. I must go and get back to your car before they arrive. Somebody will come and take a formal statement from you later. Once again, be careful . . .'

'You are not going down to the inn on your own,' Beth said shakily as we entered the kitchen. 'I don't want to sit here and wonder whether somebody's bowling you over with a Land-Rover or something.'

'I wanted you to come along anyway,' I said. 'Not for that reason – I can't see you stopping a Land-Rover by sheer willpower and there'd be no point our both getting run over. But you might get more out of Mr Wentworth than I would.'

That, apparently, was different. Beth looked terrified. 'Me? I wouldn't know how to question somebody.'

'You have a natural talent for wheedling information out of people,' I said.

'Only you.'

'And Henry and a dozen others I can think of. Also, he's rather less likely to give you a punch up the nose.'

'Thank you very much indeed,' Beth said in a hollow voice. 'That's exactly what I wanted to be told.'

'I'll find a seat near by and leap to your defence if I have to.'

'I'd rather put my trust in Jason.'

Jason was her personal Labrador. 'That soft lump?' I said. 'I suppose he could give an attacker a nasty lick.'

Beth had been messing about with crockery. She gave me a mug of coffee and sat down opposite me. 'But Mr Wentworth wouldn't know that. Jason looks fierce, that's the main thing.'

'And I don't?' I felt mildly insulted. I had certainly been in more fights than had Jason.

'Anyone could see at a glance that you're a pussy cat,'

Beth said. 'And you don't look strong. How on earth would I open the subject? I can't just walk up to the man and ask him if he killed his wife and a tramp.'

'No. But you could ask him if he isn't missing a puppy,' I suggested.

Beth thought about it and then nodded. 'I suppose I could. All right. At least you can buy me my lunch. Wait a minute while I organize things.'

While I waited, I phoned Foleyknowe House and explained to an answering machine that due to a mishap with a car, I was without transport for the moment. Unless I heard to the contrary, I would come at the planned time but on the morrow.

Beth's minute stretched to nearly an hour while she attended to Sam, arranged with Daffy for his care over lunchtime, and changed into clothing more suitable for lunching out, but it was my guess that we had time to spare.

We walked down to the village, but we took a footpath that ran behind the houses and brought us out near the inn and almost opposite the police station.

'It may be over by now,' Beth said as we walked.

'You mean, Wentworth may have confessed?'

'No, silly. I meant the championship.'

I had forgotten about the big event of the spaniel year, but suddenly I could see it all in my mind. A slow-motion dance of nervous handlers and excited dogs among the walkers, the spectators, sporting journalists and photographers, judges, Guns, and stewards. Dogs being put out for speaking, for unsteadiness, for running jealous, or for missing game. Other dogs being called forward again for one more run while the handlers' hopes rose. Then an anxious wait, probably in the rain, bladders ready to burst with anxiety and cold, while the judges conferred. Triumph and disappointment and a general move towards the nearest bar or telephone. I did not miss the tension of top-level competition, but I found that I was missing the atmosphere.

'They'll go on all afternoon,' I said.

'For the look of it. But the judges will have made their minds up by now.'

'I doubt it very much.' I had done some judging and sometimes I had not really made up my mind until a week after the awards had been given out and everybody had gone home.

Outside the Police House a lanky figure was hosing traces of dung off the official Escort. A rising and gusting wind was blowing spray around, making rainbows in the weak sunshine. 'You go on in,' I said. 'I'll have a word with Constable Peel and catch up with you.'

Beth nodded. 'Keep Jason with you.'

I snapped my fingers to bring Jason to heel and crossed the street. Peel finished a careful sluicing under the wings and turned off the hose. 'I've called the service station,' he said. 'They said they'll collect the car, but how they'll get it out of there without it running away God alone knows.'

'That's their problem,' I said. 'Theirs and the insurers.' I lowered my voice. 'How's the interview going?'

'Finished.' Peel's voice was barely a murmur. 'He went over to the inn for a bar lunch a few minutes ago. I had a word with the sergeant. Wentworth claimed to have an alibi, but he slept alone in an Inverness hotel the night his wife was killed and he could have sneaked out and driven both ways in the time available.'

'Did anybody see him, or anybody like him, in the bar at Hogmanay?'

Peel raised his eyes for a moment to the heavens. 'Did you ever try asking somebody – who's been drinking – who he saw in a crowded bar? By the time I was taken off the case we'd pegged most of the crowd and eliminated nearly all of them. Not less than three men and not more than seven – depending on whether or not the witnesses are describing the same ones – were unaccounted for but, of those, at least one had left while Dinnet was still on the scrounge.'

'I'll take a look at Wentworth and see if he rings any bells.' A Land-Rover weaved uncertainly down the street. 'That's Harvey Welcome,' I said. 'He was in the bar that night. I've just remembered. I might have a word with him.'

'I'll be having the word with him,' Peel said. 'You needn't bother. Apart from the drink he'd taken, he wasn't wearing his contact lenses that evening, so the only way he recognized people was by their voices. And by the look of his driving he's not wearing them now. It's time I gave him another Last Warning.'

As I crossed the road, I was deciding not to take any more action just yet. Beth and I would take the promised look at Mr Wentworth. Whether or not we recognized him, we would let the police know and then leave it to them. They had the resources and it seemed that they also had more than one suspect. Time enough to neglect my work and endanger my family when their attention was focused again on Angus.

All the same, I entered the inn through the back door. It was not much out of my way. There were two old-series short-chassis Land-Rovers in the car park. Each was battered-looking and rusty around the front bumper. One was muddy but the other had recently been washed and polished.

It was still early for lunch but, the day being Saturday, there was a small throng of drinkers in the large and rambling bar. I recognized a farmer who had been in the bar at Hogmanay but had left early. The muddier of the two Land-Rovers would be his.

Beth, a half-pint of shandy in her hand, was sharing a small table with a fair-haired man, in tweeds of too bright a check for one of his height, who was working his way through one of the inn's individual steak pies. Low eyebrows and a turned-down mouth gave him a naturally peevish expression but Beth's presence did not seem to have improved his mood.

I took a stool at the end of the bar, within about six

114

feet of them. Jason settled at my feet. Years of close acquaintance with firearms had spoiled my hearing at certain wavelengths, but when the conversations further along the bar were not too boisterous I could make out most of what they were saying. Lip-reading in the mirror behind the bar helped.

'No, I'm not from the media,' Beth was saying, with a merry little laugh that rang almost true. 'Do I look like a media person?'

I missed most of the reply. Wentworth was facing partly away from me. His voice did not carry as well as Beth's higher tones and Florrie had come to take my order. I asked for the scampi and a pint of Guinness.

'. . . won't want to talk to strangers during your hour of grief,' I heard Beth say.

There was a lull in the other conversations and the man's voice came through clearly, low and hostile. 'You're right. I don't want to talk to strangers. Who are you, to be asking questions? You're not just interested in some damn puppy.'

'Just curious,' Beth said weakly.

'Curious be damned!' Wentworth's voice was rising to match his anger.

Beth swallowed. 'All right, I'll tell you. I think my husband may have been visiting her. He was supposed to be bringing home a puppy.'

'What sort of puppy?' he asked.

'I don't know.' Beth managed to sound almost tearful.

Wentworth paused and when he spoke again his tone had softened and his voice had fallen lower. 'That's tough. I don't know that I can say much to help you.'

'I only want to be sure,' Beth said plaintively. 'Anything you can tell me, in confidence, might help set my mind at rest.'

Wentworth sighed. 'I don't want anybody to get the wrong ideas. The stupidest thing I could do just now would be to try to give the impression that my late wife and I were all lovey-dovey when half the world knows that the honeymoon was long gone. So I'll tell you what I've just been telling the police. We were due for a divorce. I have another lady in mind and she had a lover, but I don't know who he was. It suited us to go on sharing the house until one or other of us was ready to make the break.

'I'm sick to my heart at the way she went. I'd be sorry for anyone who died that way and I'll never get over the jolt it gave me, finding her like that.' His voice cracked for a moment. 'I don't know that it'll ever be far from my mind and if I marry again I'll never want to see my new wife in the bath. But this isn't my "hour of grief", as you put it.'

Beth's voice was partly swamped by laughter at the other end of the bar and Florrie distracted me by putting my pint in front of me and telling me conversationally that a big wind was forecast. When I had got rid of her without hurting her feelings more than slightly, I could hear Beth again.

'. . . have the puppy safe not very far from here. You're quite sure that he isn't yours?'

'I've told the police a dozen times and I'll tell you once and for all,' Wentworth said. 'I loathe dogs. I'd sooner have a diarrhoeic goat in the house. Satisfied?'

Beth pretended to misunderstand. 'If your wife knew that you hated dogs, why did she get a puppy? Was it just to upset you?'

There was a pause. In the mirror, I saw Wentworth chew and swallow. 'I'm damn sure that she didn't get any such thing. She knew that I'd have got rid of it in no time flat. Not by stamping on it, mind. Finding a dead puppy in the hall gave me a hell of a shock, but it was only the beginning . . . No, I'd have got the RSPCA to take it away. And, if she had been daft enough to buy a puppy, knowing how I feel about dogs, she wouldn't have got a spaniel. That wasn't her scene at all, tweeds and waxproofs and green wellies. She was a very elegant lady and she made sure that she came across that way. She enjoyed her elegancies. A borzoi or a saluki would have been more her thing.'

'Perhaps her lover,' Beth suggested. 'Was he the sort of man . . .?' Her voice tailed away. I decided that she was showing a remarkable talent for interrogation.

'How the hell would I know?' Wentworth demanded angrily. 'I knew that there was somebody but I didn't know who and I didn't want to know and I still don't. Frankly, I had more important things to think about, like whether I needed a new toothbrush. She was discreet about it, I'll say that for her, and that's all that mattered. But an old biddy who spends her time peeping from behind the lace curtains at the dead end road up to my house insisted on telling me whenever my wife had been entertaining while I was away on business.'

'Has she described him to the police?'

Wentworth drained his beer glass and signalled to Florrie for his bill. 'After a fashion,' he said. 'Same man each time, she's sure, but it could have been anybody from your husband to the local minister.'

'Did he come in a Land-Rover?'

'Sometimes. But sometimes in a car she didn't recognize except to say that it looked expensive. You'd better ask her for yourself if you want to eliminate your husband's car.'

'Perhaps I should,' Beth said. 'Did she say whether the lover was there the night your wife died?'

It seemed to me to be a reasonable question for a worried wife to ask but it hit the wrong note with Wentworth. He stood up and towered over Beth. 'Who the hell are you? I didn't get a name. What are you after?'

Beth, visibly uncertain how to go on, looked at me. I would have liked to see how she coped, but Wentworth's deep anger was nearing the surface again and it was quite possible that he was a serial killer. I decided to intervene before she gave away our identities. I slipped off my stool and came up behind Wentworth, clicking my fingers to bring Jason to heel. 'So this is the man you've been sneaking away to meet,' I growled to Beth.

Wentworth spun round and met the most ferocious expression that I could assume. He was beginning to flare up when he looked down to see Jason sniffing at his leg. He turned on his heel and walked away quickly.

'There goes somebody who doesn't think I look like a pussy cat,' I said.

'He was running away from Jason,' Beth said indignantly. 'He said that he hated dogs. Can I have the gammon steak?'

While Beth ate her gammon steak, I had another pint and a word with the landlord. He and the barmaids had been questioned over and again by the police, but none of them could be sure who had been in the bar at around the time of the fatality, let alone who left on the heels of the unfortunate Dinnet. To them, when the bar was busy, the customers were voices ordering drinks and hands delivering money. The landlord rather thought that Angus had still been around until he was ready to lock up. One of the part-time barmaids, who had been on duty at Hogmanay and was serving again in the public bar, remembered seeing Angus in deep discussion with a strange – in the sense of 'unfamiliar' – gentleman who I presumed was Mr de Forgan, but she had no idea when the stranger had departed and her description was so vague that I was left without any mental picture of him at all.

As we came out of the inn the service station's recovery vehicle went by, towing Henry's car and followed by a police Range Rover.

We set off for home by the path behind the houses. Beth had to raise her voice to be heard in the rising wind. 'That didn't do us much good,' she said. 'But he's one of our best suspects so far, isn't he?'

'Apart from Angus,' I said.

'I could sooner believe in Mr Wentworth as a murdering sadist than in Angus.'

'You'd suspect anybody who didn't like dogs,' I told her. 'Sadism is very much a suppressed emotion. Our murderer will probably turn out to be known as a gentle soul, kind to animals and noted for taking comforts to

118

the sick. There were concentration-camp guards in Nazi Germany who sang sentimental songs about their mothers with tears in their eyes.'

'Oh.' Beth thought that over in silence. 'We're not getting on very well, are we?' she said at last.

'No, we're not,' I said. 'The police have all the skills and facilities and manpower that we lack. I think we've got to wait and shoot holes in their case if they finally pick on Angus. But I doubt if Angus will need much help from us. And I think that the murderer is somebody quite different.'

'So do I. Who do you suspect?'

'I don't know.'

'Then I don't know what you're on about,' she said peevishly.

I pulled her out of the wind into the shelter of a clump of holly. 'Forensic science has come a long way in the last few years,' I said. 'Sometimes it can point a finger at the culprit, but not usually. I mean, the scientist can't find a hair or a fibre or some other faint trace and say, "Charlie Jones did this deed." What happens more often is that routine produces the suspect. After that, forensic science can usually prove conclusively whether he's guilty or not.

'In this case, they have a coat which can be assumed to belong to the murderer. You can be pretty sure that hairs and fibres from the coat have been passed under the microscope. Ditto hairs and fibres traceable back to Angus, Mr Wentworth, and any other good suspects. There would have been an arrest by now if any of them had matched.

'That suggests to me that Wentworth is in the clear, at least as far as the running-down of Dinnet is concerned. So it seems almost certain that Mrs Wentworth was murdered by her lover rather than her husband.'

'Did you hear what he said about the cars?'

'Most of it.'

'The neighbour saw a Land-Rover,' Beth said. 'But I don't see Angus in that role. Are you warm enough?'

'I'm all right. I can imagine Angus having an affair, but even apart from what I just said I couldn't imagine an "elegant and fastidious" lady having an affair with him.'

'She might have wanted what they call "a bit of rough",' Beth suggested.

'Not that damn rough. Anyway, if he'd left detectable traces in her house he'd have been charged by now.'

'So Angus is in the clear?'

'Probably. Unless they decide to go ahead with the hit-and-run charge and keep the rest of it separate. He could have been an accomplice of Mrs Wentworth's murderer or the victim of an appalling coincidence.'

'You mean, he had a genuine accident which happened to be with the man who'd just stolen the murderer's coat?' Beth wrinkled her nose at me. 'I can't believe that.'

'I didn't say that I believed it,' I pointed out. 'But it could have happened.'

'Millions of things could have happened but most of them didn't,' Beth said. 'Come on.' She pulled me out into the wind again.

At Three Oaks, two clients were waiting and Sam was fretful. I sold a young part-trained dog and accepted a cocker spaniel for training before I was free to phone the service station. The police had released Henry's car but it would take several days, I was told, to get the parts. I begged them to make all possible speed. Henry rarely used his car, but if deprived of the use of it he was inclined to fret.

The afternoon was too blustery for normal training. The dogs were distracted by the wind and the sound of a whistle was lost in it. I resorted to the barn, teaching obedience and elementary retrieving to the youngsters and reminding the older dogs of response to hand signals.

At six, when the phone rang, I was nursing Sam and a drink in the kitchen while Beth prepared our meal. I reached for the phone and switched on the amplifier which would let Beth hear both ends of the conversation. Daffy appeared out of nowhere.

Isobel was on the line. Her voice was cheerful and only slightly slurred. 'Well, that's it over for another year.'

'With what result?'

'I can't imagine a better one for us.'

'We won?'

'No.' I could hear somebody snorting with laughter in the background. Henry or a good impersonator.

Beth and Daffy, who had broken into grins, looked shattered. Even Sam produced a whimper.

'Don't talk in riddles,' I told Isobel severely. 'Break it to us. Or go and have a black coffee and call us again. What happened?'

'Lob got second and Rowan got a Certificate of Merit,' Isobel said. The girls began to grin again. That made Lob up to champion and it was a further distinction for Rowan who had already attained that status. 'And the winner,' Isobel went on, 'was Charles Hipple with Crab. Registered name—'

'Crabapple of Throaks,' Beth and Daffy said in chorus. They linked arms and did a little dance. Crab was one of Briar's pups.

'So that's first, second, and a certificate for our stock,' Isobel said, pointing out the obvious. 'And we've made damn sure that the journalists realized it. That should be worth ten per cent on the price of a pup.'

'Well done!' I said. 'Well done indeed!' The girls were gesturing at me. 'Daffy and Beth send their congratulations too. There will be champagne when you get back. Are you staying over another night?'

'The hotel's bloody awful,' Isobel said. 'And Rex seems to be missing his oats. We're thinking of starting back and seeing how far we get.'

'There's a hell of a gale here,' I said. 'Do you have it?'

'Not yet, but it's forecast. If we run into high winds, we'll maybe find another hotel and wait it out. Your car swings about a bit in a crosswind.'

'Try to get back,' I said incautiously. 'I need the car.'

'Use Henry's.'

I had no wish to try to explain over the phone that the mishap to Henry's car had not been my fault. 'It's almost out of petrol,' I said.

121

EIGHT

The gale kept us awake during the night, soughing under the eaves and rattling flying twigs on the slates. It peaked in the early morning and then began, very slowly, to abate.

Following the sabotage to Henry's car, we had expected, at the very least, a visit from DCI Kipple and an interrogation on such subjects as where the car had stood overnight and what we could have said or done to invite such attention. In this we were disappointed. But for the arrival of a uniformed constable from Cupar, who paced around the gravel in the apparent hope that the saboteur had left behind a hacksaw or a few spanners, we could have supposed that the police were sublimely uninterested in any attempts on our lives or wellbeing.

The travellers, we learned by phone, had slept near Carlisle and were now meeting the worst of the wind. It seemed unlikely that they would be back in time for me to keep my appointment at Foleyknowe. So I phoned Angus Todd, explained my predicament, and arranged to borrow his Land-Rover. He drove it over to Three Oaks after lunch. I saw him coming and was waiting on the gravel.

'Move over,' I told him. 'I'll run you home and get the feel of this thing at the same time.'

He clambered over the gear levers into the passenger seat and I settled myself behind the wheel. The wind pushed the unstreamlined vehicle around less than I expected.

'I could come with you,' Angus said. 'I'd like to hear what you say to Mr de Forgan.'

'Better not. I want to clear up the loose ends about the shoot,' I said. 'Nothing you don't know about. After that, I'd rather you weren't there while I ask him what he'll say if you have to call him as a witness.'

'You still think it'll come to that?'

'It may,' I said carefully. 'Not about murder; but if they don't catch their murderer or can't connect him more closely with Dinnet's death, the big danger is that they might settle for the hit-and-run charge. I don't think Mr de Forgan's evidence will be useful, but we won't know that for sure if we don't ask him. That's all right, isn't it?'

'I suppose so. I said I wouldn't name him to the police, but I told him you'd be asking questions.'

'How did he react?'

'He didn't seem too fashed about it. Why don't you want me around?'

'You blow your top too damned easily. I don't want you putting his back up just because he doesn't say what you think he should say.'

Angus swallowed that without blowing his top but when I drew up at his house he sat for a moment before returning to the subject. 'Well, don't you go angering him either,' he said. 'If he takes a scunner to you, we could lose that lease. He's generally easy-going, but he can flare up.'

'I'll be the soul of tact,' I told him.

'You do that.'

Traffic on the Road Bridge and along the north side of the Tay was slowed by the wind. Large vans were crawling and a caravan had blown onto its side. By the time I turned through the gates of Foleyknowe the short afternoon of midwinter in Scotland was almost over and the sun, invisible behind dark clouds, was low in the sky.

As Mr de Forgan had suggested, I wanted another look at the ground in daylight. I bypassed the house and

123

bumped up the track to the fork. Several of the tall pines had been uprooted by the wind and lay at forlorn angles; others were listing precariously and one, I noticed, had split near the base. I parked near the shed where I thought that Angus's Land-Rover would be safe from further casualties.

My objective was the hump of hill that rose between the two valleys, but I had to make a lengthy detour rather than walk beneath the moving trunks. Pheasants moved away in front of me, but in nothing like the number that the ground could have held. Once I was clear of the trees I climbed a fence and set off up the hill, staggering sideways on the grass whenever a gust of wind hit me.

At the top, I clung to a fence post and used my watering eyes. Angus had been right. The thick hedges that separated the fields had not been replaced by wire for the sake of a few extra yards of cultivable land. It would be easy to feed the birds upward to the clumps of gorse and bracken on the hilltops where a few strips of kale would hold them for the beaters. I could see at least six good drives and a couple of alternatives. When the birds passed over the guns they would be high and travelling like bullets, worthy quarry for the most skilled and demanding of visitors. Further along one of the valleys I could see a wide patch of bogland which could be worked up for woodcock or snipe.

I made my way down again in failing light, glad to get out of the worst of the wind. The saplings on the low ground were reaching up out of their guards and due for a burst of growth. One more year would see a transformation.

Back at the Land-Rover, I looked at my watch. I was still rather early for my appointment with Mr de Forgan. I decided to take another and longer look at the shed, check it again for dampness and try to envisage it holding the feed, traps, tools, pen sections, and all the paraphernalia of keepering, with room to spare for Angus's little All-Terrain Vehicle.

When I pushed the shed door it opened again, rather more easily than before. Something drew my attention downwards and I noticed that the doorpost had been repaired but that the door had been left unlocked. I was wondering whether this was the owner's way of inviting me to take a look inside when a voice spoke behind me.

'Yes,' it said. 'I thought you wouldn't be able to resist poking your long nose in here again.'

I began to turn with an apology already on my lips, but something heavy whacked me on the back of the head. The world turned into a whirlpool of pain and I went down hard on my face.

I was stunned but I never quite lost consciousness. Through an enveloping cloud of pain I was aware, as if from a great distance, that somebody had lifted my underweight frame without any great difficulty. I was carried a few yards and dropped ungently onto damp ground which heaved like a ship at sea. There followed a squeaking sound which I was too dazed to identify.

My head was so filled with pain that I was in the dream state in which the mind becomes disembodied. The limp and nauseous form on the ground could have belonged to anybody but me. When a pair of hands gripped my wrists and dragged me along on my face, I would have been unable to resist – but in a remote corner of my mind some part of me was crawling back towards reality and insisted that I had been hit by a flying branch and that some friend was dragging me to safety.

I was grateful to be left alone for a few seconds. All that I wanted in the world was to be left to sleep off what was either concussion or the most monstrous hangover the world had ever seen. I tried to snuggle down into a bed of earth and stone and dead pine needles.

There was a groan which was not all mine as a monstrous weight descended on my back. The breath was crushed out of me. The few functioning cells of my brain nudged their neighbours into sluggish activity but I could not understand, except that I knew now how a stranded

125

fish must feel. If I did not breathe soon I would die.

With a great effort, I opened my eyes. Somebody was kneeling down and looking into my face. He put his hand over my nose and mouth for a second and then backed away.

I turned my head, more in a desperate search for air than to try to make sense of a world gone mad, and I saw that I was lying under one of the fallen trees. The tree was across my back and it was this that was crushing me to death. The light and my consciousness were ebbing fast but some feet away I could see the figure of the man, still kneeling. He was fiddling with something under the trunk. He pumped a handle twice and a little of the weight came off me. I could just begin to breathe again, almost but not quite enough for life.

'That's better,' he said. He got up, brushed his knees and I felt a fractional increase in the load on my back as he took a seat on the fallen tree.

A little more of my mind came back to life, pushing aside the pain. A hydraulic car jack, that's what it was. And although the man was now out of my sight I remembered the face looking into mine. I had seen him before, somewhere, and his voice was not unfamiliar. I had heard it, and not on the phone.

He was speaking – to me, I realized suddenly. 'Whatever the media call me,' he said, 'I'm not a sadist. But nor do I believe in turning the other cheek. Only weaklings do that. When somebody has managed to make me bloody angry, I hit back. And I give them time to wish that they'd stayed a long way out of my way. That's all.' He was speaking calmly and quietly so that it was difficult to hear his words over the wind in the trees.

My mind was functioning again at about half throttle. I wanted to ask him what I'd ever done to incur his anger, but I needed all my breath and more. I could only expand my chest a few millimetres, but I had discovered that I could use my stomach muscles to force up my diaphragm and keep the life-giving air going in and out. For the moment, that was the summit of my ambition.

'That Wentworth bitch,' he said. 'I was sick to death of her and there was somebody else by then. We'd enjoyed each other for a year but I found her wanting. Always wanting. Wanting money. Wanting presents. Wanting sex. And then wanting me to divorce my wife and marry her. I'd told her from the beginning that that was out of the question. I'd been honest with her but she'd been stringing me along. When I told her that we were through, she threatened to go to my wife. I couldn't have that. I love my family.'

The light was almost gone. Out of the corner of my eye I could barely distinguish the silhouette of his legs among the shapes of the trees. It was a reasonable bet that if I could not see him he could not make out my shape against the dark ground. My elbows were hampered by the tree trunk but without abandoning my fight for breath I managed to feel around me.

The dispassionate voice droned on. 'Todd told me that you were helping him but I never thought that you'd be a danger to me, not even although we'd met. When Todd told me that you were to be his partner, I decided to break off negotiations about the lease. But before I could find a good reason for that, I saw you from the house. You were nosing around. And you had those cocker spaniel bitches in the back of your car. I couldn't recognize them, but they had to be the same ones. Why else would a breeder of springers have three black cockers with him? When you forced your way into the shed I knew that you were real trouble. That's when I remembered what I'd said. I had been careless.'

Between my concussion, the struggle for breath, and the total unreality of what was happening to me, my mind was in a nightmare of confusion; yet parts of my consciousness were working independently. I could recognize the mentality of the psychopath, apparently rational and sometimes brilliant but quite unable to see any obligations of morality beyond his own desires. They turn up regularly in the Forces and, for as long as the disciplines of the service hold, they can be valuable. Some earn

127

decorations, often posthumously. And, as I had suggested to Beth, many of them have a soft spot for kittens, children, or grandmothers. Somewhere, the circuits are incomplete.

To my right, the gap between the tree trunk and the ground narrowed, made smaller by a bulge of immovable rock. To my left was almost as bad, except that another slight hump in the ground, also of rock, was smaller and something in its shape suggested that it might be loose. Still breathing frantically from the diaphragm, I began scrabbling with my left hand, heedless of broken nails but careful to work in silence and to send no telltale vibrations through the timber. It was cold but at least I was down out of the worst of the wind.

'That's a good little pup you sold me,' he said. 'I owe you something for that. I'm not superstitious as a rule, but there was a curse on those bloody cockers. If only I'd known . . .

'I was on my way home with the first one when I called to see Vi Wentworth. Well, I know what pups are. Rather than leave him to panic and chew up the inside of a bloody expensive car I slipped him into my pocket where he quickly went to sleep. She doesn't – didn't – have anywhere to hang a coat in the hall so I laid my coat carefully over a chair. How was I to know that the little bugger would wake up and wriggle out? When I came downstairs after – you know? – I wasn't thinking about the pup, I was thinking about her, up there with the cold water rising and wishing that she'd never tried to threaten me. I stepped right on him in the dark. If I'd had the stomach for it, I'd have taken the body away, although the mess would still have been there to tell the tale. But I'd fallen for the pup and I couldn't bring myself to touch it.' He was speaking very quietly, in a conversational voice, as much to himself as to me. That alone was shocking, as if my doctor had slipped in the revelation of an incurable cancer between discussions of the weather. De Forgan's tone was petulant and distant in turn but, when he spoke of his victim waiting to drown in the rising water, there was a note of relish which made my flesh creep.

My scrabbling in the loose compost of pine needles unearthed a sliver of slate and I began to use that as a small trowel. The embedded stone was larger than I had thought.

'When I make up my mind to do something I go ahead with it and God help anybody who gets in my way! I told my family that the pup had trodden on some broken glass and I'd had to leave it with the vet. I knew that there was another pup available and I went back for it at Hogmanay. I always carry a First Aid box in the car. I made a nick in his foot and put in a couple of stitches. I don't think that he even felt it.

'I'd promised to meet Angus Todd in the bar. My wife had the Jag so I was using the Land-Rover. I'd got hold of a pet carrier by then. The pup couldn't have done much damage in that, but when I tried to leave him on his own he began to squeal. I didn't want some well-meaning idiot coming into the bar and shouting that there was a pup in distress in a Land-Rover outside. And I'm soft about animals. He sounded so miserable that I couldn't bring myself to leave him. So once again I put him in my pocket. Lightning, I thought, never strikes twice in the same place, and anyway I was only going to be there for a few minutes and I intended to keep my coat on. But it was warm in the bar, the pup had fallen asleep, and even if he woke up I couldn't see him escaping from the pocket of a hanging coat. Also, the coat would be where I could keep an eye on it.

'Who would have expected that senile delinquent to take a fancy to my coat while I was looking the other way?' he asked indignantly of the empty air.

'I followed him up in the Land-Rover. I did what I did on the spur of the moment and it's too late to change anything now. I was going to stop and walk back for my coat, and collect the pup if it was still in one piece, but in my mirror I saw more people against the street lights of the village so I drove on.

'Later, I phoned the breeder but there were no more pups to be had. I didn't give her my name but she let me know that she recognized my voice and she was curious. The purchase of one cocker pup would have meant nothing. Two plus an enquiry for a third would have been remembered. She was the type to talk and sooner or later somebody would have connected it up. She had to go.

'I told my family that the pup had an infection and would probably have to be put down. But I'd promised them a spaniel and a spaniel they were going to have. I came to see you. If the police were accepting the thief's death as a hit-and-run accident, I might still have got my hands on the second pup, one way or the other. I got you to show me around, hoping to find out where he was being kept. Instead, I fell for the springer you showed me. It all made sense. As the owner of a springer pup it was less likely that anyone would associate me with cockers.'

The light was gone now. The stone came loose under my hand. I pushed it aside and scraped away more dirt from around the hole. The cold of the ground tried to bite into me but the work was keeping me warmed and I found my thick clothing more of a nuisance than a comfort. Inch by inch I slid and wriggled and worked my way sideways and found that I could breathe almost with ease although I was caught by the waist and neither my hips nor my chest would pass through the gap. I grasped the stone and tried to pass its unwieldy weight across my back from one hand to the other. Between the effort and the sound as a gust of stronger wind swayed the trees above us, I lost a few words.

'. . . can't stay here talking all day,' he said, for all the world as though breaking off a casual chat in the street. 'I'll make it easy for you and let it down suddenly. You were having a look around, just as we'd agreed, weighing up the shooting prospects, and the last tree to fall caught you across your back. Too bad, but these things happen.'

I would have spoken, tried to reason with him, but I had the wits to see that I must not let him know that I had any breath to spare.

He got up and stooped to let down the jack. I had no need to fake the sudden grunt of pain and expelled air. He treated me to a quick flash of a torch – more than anything, I think, to make sure that I had not written anything in the dirt. Then he walked away.

NINE

His plan deserved to succeed. If my back had not broken, I would have suffocated. Somebody would have had to use another jack to lift the tree off my body and any marks that he had left in the bark would have been attributed to that. It would have taken an observant investigator to read anything in the signs that contradicted his story. A painstaking pathologist might have noticed that the bruise on my head had preceded death by half an hour or so, but the circumstances would have been so plain that any post-mortem examination would have been cursory.

But I had managed to take two tiny steps in the direction of survival. I had squeezed sideways to where there was a little more space at my disposal. And I had jammed the loose stone between the rock and the tree trunk. The crushing weight of the tree returned, no heavier than it had been in the beginning, but now that my stomach was in the dip I had made I was arched backwards. Breathing from the diaphragm was an almost impossible feat but it was essential.

I still had the fragment of slate in my hand. I resumed my scraping at the earth beside and below me, working for a deeper hole that would let me breathe even if I could not crawl out of the trap.

The ground was stony and soon I was reduced to digging out one small stone at a time and rolling it aside. The task was hopeless. I would first have to excavate a hole and then work under my body in order to get room

132

to move. The work demanded breath that I did not have but at least it gave me some hope and a defence against the creeping chill.

I seemed to have made no progress at all when I realized that another danger was looming. My old reaction to stress was taking over. All that I wanted to do was to sleep but, if I relaxed even for a moment, the conscious effort of breathing would stop and I would never wake up again. I dragged myself back towards wakefulness and scrabbled on with my piece of slate. I might as well have tackled the Channel Tunnel with a child's bucket and spade, but I had to go on or accept death.

Time ceased to have any meaning. The scene had become static or else an endless loop. Scratch, scratch, scratch in the darkness, always one-handed, breathe from the stomach, ignore the cramps in my twisted body, dislodge a small stone, and start again. I asked myself once whether life itself was worth such a prodigious effort, but when I remembered Beth and Sam and the new life we had made for ourselves I called on reserves of willpower that I never knew I had and scrabbled on.

If I had lost consciousness I would have lost the battle for life. I must have been very close to blacking out because when I saw light and heard voices I paid them no attention but worked on, trying to make a dip into which I could slide away from that killing pressure. There were feet in front of my face. Somebody galloped away and came back. Then a jack was being pumped and the weight on my body became less and less until I found myself breathing in great gasps.

Hands grasped my wrists and pulled me out from under the tree trunk. I curled up into a ball, content to relieve the strain on my stomach muscles and to gulp in lungfuls of precious air. Beth's voice was asking questions but for the moment I was beyond answering.

At last I felt strong enough to try to roll on to my knees. The hands lifted me gently to my feet. My every muscle seemed to have been stretched and my joints wrenched almost apart. The lights of Angus's Land-Rover had been switched on and I saw another vehicle which I recognized as my own car. Beth was supporting me on one side. On the other, what I had first supposed to be the product of my feverish imagination turned out to be Rex, complete with Mohican haircut and a fringed leather jacket emblazoned with symbols of some voodoo cult.

A third person, a woman standing apart, was a stranger to me. Beth aimed a few words at her which I failed to catch and then I was bundled into the blessed warmth of my car.

'Morgan was de Forgan,' I said. My voice came thickly but it was a joy to have it back.

The sentence sounded like nonsense after I had got it out but Beth took it in her stride. 'I'd already guessed that,' she said. 'Shall I take you to Ninewells Hospital?'

'No,' I said. I had had more than enough of hospitals for one lifetime. 'I've no damage that rest won't put right.' Or, if I had, another day would be time enough. I wanted to be at home with Beth, where things were comfortable and familiar.

Something else was on my mind. 'He said—' I began.

'Yes?'

There was a pause while I sorted de Forgan's words out in my mind. 'He said he'd let something slip when he came to buy the pup. And he said that he knew I was a danger to him when he saw me looking in the shed.'

'Did he indeed? Just a minute.'

Beth, who had settled herself in the driver's seat and started the engine, got out of the car again and spoke to Rex. Then she came back, buckled her seat belt carefully and drove off. She went very slowly as far as the gates, but when the lights of Angus's Land-Rover came up behind us she accelerated away and headed for home or the police or a hospital or somewhere, I was past caring. I was deadly tired and I seemed to have said everything worth saying, so I let myself slide into darkness.

*

134

My sleep was like floating in a black pit full of nothingness, but I drifted near the surface from time to time. Once, I was being helped up some stairs, in a void that held the familiar smells of home. Then I seemed to be in my own bed and somebody who sounded like Beth was adding hot-water bottles just where I needed them.

Minutes later, it seemed, I drifted towards the surface again and there was daylight there. I turned over and let myself float. I was stiff and sore and there was a new ache in my back, but I had felt worse after an Interservices Rugby match.

Somebody had left the room. I came wide awake. The bedroom door was standing open. I was wondering whether I could be bothered to get up and do something about it when Beth came awkwardly in. She was balancing a tray in one hand while over the other arm she had my shot-gun. I sat up and took the tray.

'How do you feel?' Beth asked me.

'Not too bad, considering,' I told her. 'For once, I seem to have escaped any serious after-effects of being cold. I must be on the mend.'

'More likely you're still awash with all the dope from last time.' Beth put the gun down on the bedside table. She saw me looking at it. 'It was there all night,' she said. 'And Henry's downstairs now with his own gun. That man's had two goes at you already and a third time is not going to be lucky for him if I know anything about it. I'd rather be gaoled for shooting him than have you killed.'

'Thank you,' I said politely. 'I appreciate the thought.' The tray held tea, toast, and a boiled egg, my favourite breakfast when off-colour. I had not eaten since my light lunch the previous day. Suddenly breakfast seemed more important than a lot of questions.

'Thank God you're eating!' Beth said. She put a cool hand on my forehead. 'I thought you were going to be all right when you didn't sweat in the night, but the doctor's going to look in later.'

'I'm fine,' I said. 'Have you told the police about this?'

'Not yet. It would have sounded like a wild accusation

135

unless you could back it up, and I wasn't going to have you badgered until you'd recovered.'

'Bless you! How did you come to turn up in the nick of time?'

Beth sat lightly on the edge of the bed. 'I was beginning to wonder why you hadn't come home when the car turned up with Henry and Isobel and Rex. They were telling me all about the championship when the phone rang and it was Angus, wanting to know if you were back and how you'd got on. That was the first time I knew that you'd gone to Foleyknowe on your own. I'd thought that Angus was with you and two of you together would be all right.

'I phoned the Foleyknowe number and only got the answering machine. I was sure that I recognized the voice on the tape. It was nearly dark and I knew that you'd be indoors by then. So I got Rex to come with me and we drove to Foleyknowe. I was almost sure that I was making a fuss about nothing, and yet I knew for certain that something was wrong.' She paused. 'That sounds daft, now that I've said it.'

'I can understand it, even if you can't,' I said.

'There was no sign of Angus's Land-Rover at the house so we went on up to where we'd parked before. And there you were,' she ended triumphantly. 'Rex was just great.'

I had finished the egg but there was some toast left and I found a small pot of marmalade on the tray. Beth watched with satisfaction as I put it to good use. She looked like a shy teenager but I reminded myself that she was a mature and intelligent woman.

'But what made you sure that something was wrong? Why were you so suspicious of de Forgan?' I asked. My mouth was full and on the word 'suspicious' I spluttered some crumbs over the bedclothes. 'You never said anything,' I added.

Beth seemed to be preoccupied with picking up the crumbs. 'It was only a thought,' she said.

'So were any of the world's most brilliant ideas.'

'Well, I didn't want to confuse you. You knew as much as I did. In fact you knew more. You've been very good about telling me all about what everybody said, but that isn't the same as hearing it for yourself.

'I nearly suggested him when we were walking back from the inn and you said that you thought it would turn out to be somebody else and I said that I thought so too, and to cut a short story long . . . Or do I mean the other way around?'

'I think you had it right first time,' I said. 'Go on.'

'De Forgan . . . Morgan. The names were so similar that if he'd met you again he could easily have said that you'd misheard him. I'd wondered all along about the man Angus was to meet and then we heard that it was Mr de Forgan. Angus was so keen to get the shoot that as far as he was concerned Mr de Forgan was above suspicion but . . . when he came here, calling himself Morgan, I was at the door, remember?'

'Yes.'

'He mentioned the road fatality and referred to the dead man as a jewel thief. The papers reported the death but they hadn't said anything like that. And poor Mr Dinnet wasn't a jewel thief. The jewellery found on him had been in the pockets of the stolen coat. And who would know that, except the murderer? I suppose he'd taken back his presents to her. I call that a bit thick,' Beth added, as though recovering his presents had been a worse sin than the murder. 'Cold blooded! Then, when you phoned Mr de Forgan, he said something about the "death of a petty crook".'

'I'm not complaining,' I said. 'In fact, I'm more than grateful. But that seems a bit tenuous to send you galloping around the country to the rescue.'

'I hadn't quite finished,' Beth said sternly. 'You should try to listen more. What I've said so far is about what set me wondering. So when Angus phoned and told me that you'd gone on your own, I asked him a few questions off my own bat.

'You see, what had been bothering me all along was

about Angus's Land-Rover. You were assuming that somebody ran over Mr Dinnet with another Land-Rover and then swapped bumpers with Angus. But Angus washed his Land-Rover thoroughly on Ne'erday. He wouldn't have missed the bumper. So the bumpers must have been swapped over later.

'I asked Angus about it and he said that most of the time either he was using the Land-Rover or it was locked in his shed. Except once.

'When Mr Crae had the shooting at Foleyknowe from Mr de Forgan, Angus was keepering there and he lived in the keeper's cottage. The de Forgan children and Mrs Todd became very close. So Mrs de Forgan used to leave them with Mrs Todd whenever it suited her, and she went on doing that after the Todds moved over here. She left them with Mrs Todd on Ne'erday. In fact, Angus said that they helped him to wash the Land-Rover.

'Angus told me that they left the Land-Rover standing out to dry. Mr de Forgan came to fetch the children after dark in his own Land-Rover. I think that he'd already slacked off the bolts on his own bumper and that's when he exchanged bumpers with Angus Todd.'

I found that I was nodding. Even if we lacked proof we now had an alternative explanation for the stains on Angus's bumper, if he ever came to trial. But something still bothered me. 'He'd have been taking a hell of a risk, driving around with Dinnet's blood on his Land-Rover,' I pointed out.

'Perhaps he hadn't used the Land-Rover since he killed Mr Dinnett and he only noticed the blood and hair just before setting off. It wasn't much of a risk, driving from Foleyknowe to Angus's home in the dark. He'd have been hoping for a chance to swap bumpers with Angus – or anybody else. He'd have been much safer if the police had a conviction instead of a mystery.'

'You should have told the police about this.'

She shook her head. 'I wanted to discuss first what we were going to say to them.'

'But he's still running around loose. He'll know by now that I didn't die. God alone knows what he'll try next.' Something else was nagging at me. 'I seem to remember a woman there last night.'

'Mrs de Forgan. She turned up while we were getting you out from under that tree.'

'Does she know about her husband? Has she been protecting him?'

'I don't know. She seemed to be genuinely puzzled. I sent her packing anyway.'

There was a rap at the door. Beth's hand made an involuntary gesture, quickly checked, towards the shot-gun. 'Come in,' she called

Isobel's head came round the door. 'You're all right?' she asked me.

'No problems,' I said, 'except that I'm stiff and sore. Well done, the championship results.'

Isobel came inside the doorway. She waved away my congratulations. 'Of course, I don't know a tenth of what happened last night,' she said.

'What happened was—' Beth began.

'Tell me later. There's somebody downstairs, wanting to see John. Mrs de Forgan. I put her in the sitting room and lit the fire.'

Beth got up quickly and went to the window. 'The Jaguar,' she said to me.

'It would be,' I said. 'We'd have heard the Land-Rover.' I glanced at Isobel. 'Nobody with her in the car?'

Isobel looked blank. 'Not a soul,' she said.

'All the same . . .' Beth said. She picked up my shot-gun. 'I'd better see her.'

Ignoring a myriad twinges, I struggled out of bed in a hurry and took it out of her hands.

'You can't go down waving a gun around,' Isobel said. 'And Henry's already sitting in the kitchen making like the Spirit of Fort Apache.'

I found that I was steady on my feet. 'I'm coming with you,' I told Beth. And to Isobel, 'Tell Henry to come in quickly if he hears any loud voices. And . . . would you mind making coffee and getting out some biscuits?'

Isobel knew that I would never have treated her as a servant without good reason. She nodded and went out. I shrugged into my warm dressing-gown and found my slippers.

'We are not giving that woman coffee,' Beth said indignantly. 'Her husband's a murderer. He tried to kill you last night.'

'The coffee's mostly for me. I'm still hungry.'

Beth threw up her hands in despair. 'That's different,' she said.

Downstairs in the sitting room, where a log fire was glowing in the grate, Mrs de Forgan was waiting composedly, arranged rather than seated in one of the wing-chairs. She was a woman in her thirties, very self-assured and with the square jaw to suit. Her dress, her hair, and a few touches of costume jewellery suggested both taste and money. A coat of expensive fur had been laid across the window table with a handbag on top of it. I could tell at first glance that she was a formidable lady. If Beth had indeed 'sent her packing', the fur might have flown.

I paused just inside the door. 'I'm sure you'll excuse my *déshabillé*,' I said, choosing my words, 'but I expect you know some of what happened last night.'

'Yes,' she said, 'I do. I rather think that I know all of it. You're all right?'

By then, I was becoming tired of assuring everybody that I was more or less sound. I had also decided that she did not intend a physical mischief. I came forward, without offering to shake her hand, and took a seat on the settee. Beth joined me. Isobel had already put a tray with coffee on the low table. Mrs de Forgan shook a well-groomed head of dark blond hair when I offered her coffee. I helped myself and poured for Beth.

'What can we do for you?' I asked her.

She was unperturbed by my bluntness. She even smiled faintly, showing very even teeth. 'Do for me? Not very much. You sold my husband a springer spaniel puppy. There seems to have been some slight confusion about names and I'd like to have it corrected on the papers. I want to make sure that his registration is in order. Also, I understand that his dam became a field-trial champion yesterday. I'd like that added to his pedigree.' She had a beautifully mellow voice and an effortless lack of accent.

This was so far from what I'd been expecting that for the moment I was struck dumb. Beth stepped into the breach. 'That should be easy,' she said. 'Who told you that Lob had been made up?'

She raised an eyebrow. 'Angus Todd, when I left the children with Mrs Todd just now. Was he mistaken?'

This time, Beth was brought up short and I had found my voice. 'He was correct,' I said. 'But . . . if you're still leaving your children with Mrs Todd, I assume that you don't think Angus is guilty of the various accusations that have been made against him?'

'I'm sure that he isn't.' She waited, but neither Beth nor I had anything to say. She looked away from us into the leaping flames and went on. 'You haven't spoken to the police today.' It was a statement rather than a question.

'Not yet,' Beth said. She started to say more and then clamped her mouth shut.

Mrs de Forgan nodded slowly. 'I came here because I wanted to meet you both. And now that I've done so, I think that we can trust each other. I ask you to believe that until last night I had no knowledge of my husband's wickedness. Uneasy feelings which I hoped were unfounded, but never the least trace of proof.'

I met Beth's eye. She gave a tiny nod. 'We can accept that,' I said. 'Provisionally.'

She looked at me consideringly and then nodded again. 'We'll go on from there,' she said. 'I think you'll come to believe me.' She gave a small sigh. 'I would have had to be stupid not to know that my husband had affairs. But he genuinely cared for his family and so I was prepared to

.ore a certain amount of straying. But I also knew his character, perhaps better than he knew himself.

'So I did have my suspicions. No,' she said quickly, 'perhaps suspicions is too strong a word. But the thought was there even though I refused to let it surface. When that woman was killed, and then the man at Hogmanay, there were enough indications to make me uneasy. Unexplained absences. Puppies that never arrived. But wondering was enough and there was always a credible explanation. I wasn't prepared to put my marriage at risk by making an accusation that might have been quite unjustified. On the other hand, if I rocked the boat I might have been the next one to drown. You understand what I mean?'

'I think we do,' I said.

'But last night, after dark, my husband came back to the house, changed his muddy clothes, and drove off. He was in his hyperactive state, a mood I recognized. Later, a car arrived and drove past the house in a hurry. I decided to walk in that direction and I saw that extraordinary young man pulling you out from under the tree. You made a convincing picture of somebody who had been caught under a falling tree.'

'But it didn't convince you?' I asked her.

'Not quite. I had walked the pup in that direction during the morning. That tree was already down. And I saw your companion look in that old shed, so when you had gone I fetched a torch and looked for myself.'

Beth had been listening in silence, knowing that something big was coming but unsure what to expect. At these words I felt her grip my wrist. 'Would you tell that to the police?' she asked.

Mrs de Forgan sat back and met our eyes. 'There is no need for that,' she said. 'I do not wish my children to grow up with any stigma attached to them – the stigma of a father who was a murderer.

'You asked what you could do for me. You never asked what I could do for you, but I'll tell you anyway. I can assure you that you're in no danger any more. You can tell the gentleman in the other front room that a bodyguard is no longer required. You see, my husband died last night in an accident. It was his habit, when having a bath, to take a radio into the bathroom with him, plugged into the mains on a long cord. He used to stand it on a tall stool beside the bath. Last night, it fell into the bath and he was electrocuted. Perhaps it's as well. He would have hated prison.'

Mrs de Forgan waited patiently, as a queen might wait, for comments. Conventional expressions of regret would have been out of place. When no comment was forthcoming she went on: 'I have just visited the police. It was obvious that you had not yet made any statement. I told them that when my husband came home at Hogmanay he seemed very upset. Next morning I found him scrubbing his Land-Rover, a task which he usually left to one of his employers at the works. The front bumper had already been removed. When I challenged him, he broke down and admitted to me that he had been involved in the hit-and-run the night before. That should let your friend Angus Todd off the hook.'

'Did they believe you?' Beth asked.

Mrs de Forgan shrugged. 'Not entirely. No, of course not. But what does that signify? They know that the man they were looking for is dead, so they're hardly likely to waste a lot of resources in looking for further proof. There may be some difficulty if the two procurators fiscal decide on enquiries before the respective sheriffs, but I am engaging a top QC to represent me.'

She looked at her watch and got up. I helped her into the fur.

'You understand, of course, that this discussion never happened. If you try to report it, I shall say that you dreamed it up between you, in an effort to pervert the course of justice.'

I followed her to the front door. She glanced down at my slippers and smiled. 'You needn't come out,' she said raciously. 'We'll be in touch. If you still want the shooting rights to Foleyknowe, you can have them. There will be no rental.'

We watched from the sitting-room window as she drove competently away.

'That last remark sounded remarkably like an attempted bribe,' I said.

'An unnecessary bribe,' said Beth. She looked at me with eyes so wide that I could see white all round the irises. 'She's right. Things are best left as they are. You know what I think?'

'You think that she killed her husband, once she was absolutely sure that he was a murderer.'

'I'm sure of it. Somebody had to. Prison would have been too good for a man like that.'

In accordance with his own philosophy, I thought that prison would have given de Forgan time for regret, but I decided not to say so. 'We'd better work out what to say to Isobel and Henry.'

'They'll be bursting with curiosity.'

'So am I,' I said. I took another biscuit. 'I can see the rest of it, but what was so special about the shed? I only looked into it to see if it would be suitable for storage. Why did that get de Forgan into a tizzy? What was in there apart from straw bales?'

'He thought that you knew much more than you did.' Beth shook her head sadly. 'You remember the young motorcyclist who was crippled and left to die? About five years ago? Angus, who was the keeper, had a row with him. So did Mr Crae, who had the sporting rights. We forgot that Mr de Forgan, who was the owner of the land, was just as likely to have a grudge against him. Behind the bales,' Beth said, 'there was a motorbike. And now, you're going back to bed. I must feed Sam.'